The Window at Willow Springs

(A Fort Payne, Alabama Story)

Jill Watson Glassco

Deep Sea Publishing, LLC

Copyright Page

The Window at Willow Springs, Copyright © 2021 by Jill Watson Glassco

Illustrations: Anya Figert

Cover Design: Ben Glassco

Cover Art: Jill Glassco

Printed in the USA

ISBN-13: 978-1-939535-45-0
ISBN: 1-939535-45-X

Table of Contents

To

Karen

Thanks for sharing Willow Springs

Chapter 1:

Williams Avenue

"The old has gone, the new is here."
(2 Corinthians 5:17)

"Repeat after me," Mrs. Robinson said. "Owa!"

"Owa!"

She raised both arms and shouted, "Tagoo!"

"Tagoo!!" we hollered.

"Siam!" she bellowed.

"Siam!!!"

Mrs. Robinson grinned. "Faster, children. Owa tagoo siam!"

"Owa tagoo siam!!"

"Faster! Owa-tagoo-siam!"

"Owa-tagoo-saim!!"

"As fast as you can! Owatagoosiam!"

"Owatagoosiam!! O wa ta goos I am!! O what a goose I am!!"

I shot my new teacher a suspicious look. "Hey, wait a minute."

Mrs. Robinson was cackling and dabbing tears from both eyes. The whole class burst out laughing. The silly-goose joke worked. My butterflies settled.

That first day of fifth grade in September of 1966 was my first day at Williams Avenue School. Over the summer, our town had reconfigured the schools, assigning first through fourth graders to Forest Avenue Elementary and the fifth through eighth graders to Williams Avenue Intermediate. The ninth through twelfth graders stayed put at Fort Payne High School (the former DeKalb County High School built in 1910 at the foot of Lookout Mountain close to Hawkins Springs).

Before the eight o'clock bell, my brother, Mark (an eighth grader), had walked me past a lunchroom with polished, white-tiled floors. He pointed left. "The fifth and sixth grade classrooms are that way, and I'm at the other end of the building. Do you remember where Mrs. Robinson's room is?"

I nodded.

"You okay?"

I nodded again and forced a smile. I wished he would walk me to the door. Anytime I got all prickly inside, Mark made me feel safe and secure.

"Who likes to read?" Mrs. Robinson held up a paperback book. The front cover showed a bare-foot girl under a sun bonnet carrying a box of berries.

7

Four other students and I raised a hand.

"Reading regularly strengthens your brain and improves brain connectivity. You may not appreciate that now, but just wait till you're my age. I'll take all the brain power I can get. What other benefits can reading offer?"

My hand shot up.

"Yes, Jill?"

"My mama's a librarian, and she said that reading increases your vocabulary and comprehension skills."

"She's absolutely right. That's why one of my top goals for you young'uns this year is to help you develop a love for reading. So, saddle up your horses, kiddos, and get ready to ride. We're going on a great adventure in the land of books."

I raised my hand again.

"Yes, Jill."

"Mama said that families who read together have more fun."

"Yes, reading together is a wonderful practice. Now, as I was saying, our first together-book is Lois Lenski's *Strawberry Girl.* This children's fiction was published in 1945 and became the 1946 Newbery Medal winner. Let the adventure begin!"

Mrs. Robinson read in a thick hillbilly accent:

"Thar goes our cow, Pa!" said the little girl.

"Shore 'nough, that do look like one of our cows, now don't it?"

The man tipped his slat-backed chair against the wall of the house. He spat across the porch floor onto the sandy yard. His voice was a lazy drawl. He closed his eyes again . . ."

At noon, we followed Mrs. Robinson to the lunchroom like ducklings behind mama duck.

"What's in there?" I asked, pointing to heavy, double doors.

"Open it and see," Nina Boyce encouraged.

I cracked the door to a gymnasium with a thick-curtained stage just as Mrs. Rotch, our no-nonsense principal, stepped out of her office catty-cornered from the gym. Her face looked stern, but her eyes were smiling. "Girls, stay with your class."

"Yes, ma'am." We hurried to catch up.

"And no running in the halls."

We slowed. "Yes, ma'am."

I jumped when the "school's-out" bell clanged and ran to the playground. Mark was sitting in a tall swing but not swinging. Tossing my plaid book satchel to the dust, I plopped into the swing beside him. "How long will it take Mama to get here from Forest Avenue?"

He shrugged.

Mama used to stay home with us three kids while Daddy practiced law. But when the elementary school principal begged her to set up a library and run it, she took the job.

"Teaching is perfect for a working mother," she explained, "because you have the same hours and vacation days as your children."

"Do you like Mrs. Robinson?"

"Yeah! She's funny. Is eighth grade fun?"

He shook his head. "Not yet."

Mark confessed that while Mr. McKay, the eighth-grade history teacher, demonstrated the Native American grass dance, he had hollered, "Go, glamour girl!"

I giggled.

"Well, Mr. McKay didn't think it was funny. He barked, 'Mark Watson, I can tell you and I are in for some trouble this year.'"

"Uh oh."

"Yeah, I know. I gotta figure out a way to get on his good side."

I traced a circle in the dirt with my tennis shoe. "Just tell him you're not a bad kid."

Mark shook his head. "Daddy says words ring hollow, but actions speak . . ."

"There's Mama." I jumped from the swing and grabbed my bookbag. In the car, I blurted, "Mark got in trouble today."

Surprise painted Mama's face. "What happened, Mark?"

He sighed. "Well, I tried to make Mr. McKay laugh, but it backfired."

Her eyes met his in the rearview mirror. "Did you apologize?"

"Yes, ma'am."

"Just work extra hard at being respectful and show him you're not a troublemaker."

"Yes, ma'am."

REFLECTIONS

A POINT TO PONDER

Why did Mr. McKay think Mark was a troublemaker?

A PEARL FROM GOD

"Brothers and sisters do not slander one another. Anyone who speaks against a brother or sister or judges them speaks against the law and judges it . . . who are you to judge your neighbor?" (James 4:11-13)

A PRINCIPLE TO LIVE BY

An old saying goes: "don't judge a book by its cover." In other words, don't judge someone by outward appearance or first impressions. Beloved, get to know a person and search for good qualities in everyone you meet.

Chapter 2:

Lookout Mountain

"I lift up my eyes to the mountains." (Psalm 121:1)

"Mama, don't go up Third Street," I begged. "Take First Street and go up the mountain by Sharon's house."

Fort Payne stretched down a narrow valley between Lookout Mountain (where I lived) and Sand Mountain in the northeast corner of Alabama. The old folks said that in its "Boom Days" of the late 1800s, investors in coal and iron flooded the valley. But when the mines fizzled out like a wet firecracker, the fortune-hunters skedaddled back north emptyhanded. Nowadays, a whole bunch of sock mills peppered our little town, making us the "Sock Capital of the World."

One time, my friend, Sharon Abbott, took me to the Fort Payne Hosiery Mill where her daddy worked. Ladies sat behind long rows of clacking knitting machines. Giant spools of thread spun around like tops.

In the warehouse, piles of boxes packed with tons of socks stacked up to the ceiling.

Mrs. Abbott worked for the mill, too, but from home in a little workroom off the garage. Sitting at a wooden table with a narrow, metal hoop bolted to the top, she stretched a sock over the hoop, trimmed off green threads, and then tossed the sock into a box to go back to the mill. Her hands flew faster than those knitting machines! I wanted to try it but didn't ask.

Sharon isn't in Mrs. Robinson's class this year. I wish she were.

At the red brick house against Lookout Mountain, Sharon stepped off the school bus, and Wiggles, her dog, barked a welcome home. I hung halfway out the window and hollered, "Hey, Sharon!"

She waved.

Mama glanced around and almost ran off the road. "Jill! Get back in the car!"

I dropped in the seat as the Ford climbed on up the mountainside. Because our family had lived along a ledge of Lookout Mountain since Rocky was two and before Mark and I were born, I knew every bump, twist, and bend in the road by heart and could have found my way home blindfolded.

Just before the horseshoe curve in the road, Mark pleaded, "Mama, please stop the car and let us climb up the bluff to the house."

"Not in your school clothes."

"We won't get dirty. Please?"

"Mark."

"Yes, ma'am."

A quarter mile past the sharp curve, Mama turned right onto the newly paved road. Until recently, it had been covered with Fort Payne chert blasted from the local quarry. The black top was ideal for biking, and the neighborhood kids thought it was the best thing to come our way since city water, which was piped in just a couple of years before.

Five small houses hugged the bluff. Our friends, Freddy and Steve Eberhart, lived in the second house. Their grandparents and aunt lived in the first house. The Raymonds along with two grumpy dogs lived in the third house, and we lived in the fourth house where the pavement ended. Another mile along the old chert road took you to the Winters' house.

"Do y'all have homework?" Mama asked.

I shook my head. "No ma'am. It's just the first day of school."

"What about you, Mark?"

"I have to write '*I will not act silly in class*' a hundred times, and I'm up to fifty-seven."

"Okay, you can finish that after supper. Y'all run change your clothes and go play."

We scrambled out of the car, charged into the house, and were back outside in two wags of a dog's tail as Daddy would say. I plucked a yellow apple from the tree by the rail fence and took a bite. "Let's go to Granddaddy Eberhart's pond," I mumbled through a mouth full of juicy fruit.

"No, let's go to Big Rock."

"Okay."

"Big Rock" was our nickname for the rocky bluff overlooking Fort Payne between our house and the Winters. I used it as a hiding place when I was sad or mad — like the time that Mama took me for a haircut, and Mr. Randall cut it so short that I looked like a boy. I was in third grade. At school the next day, after the umpteenth "Ooh, why'd you cut your hair off?" I buried my face in my arms and cried. After school, I hid. Rocky found me at Big Rock and let me bawl on his shoulder before taking me home. I wondered if Mark needed a hiding place today.

We tromped down the worn path into the woods behind the Tarzan swing in the backyard. The trail led to a stream and waterfall. The dry summer had left the falls not much more than a trickle. Mark jumped the creek. I followed. We scrambled up the other side on a path cut through thick ivy and surprised a little fieldmouse. It burrowed under the green leaves.

"Remember plantin' this ivy?" Mark said.

"Yep, I was in Mrs. Hulsey's kindergarten. Freddy and Steve helped us pull it from Mama's flowerbeds, and

I peeked sideways. Worry crinkled Mark's brow. I gave him a hug and tried to cheer him up. "It's gonna be a good year, Mark. You'll see."

"I hope so," he muttered.

REFLECTIONS

A POINT TO PONDER

What did I do when Mark felt worried?

A PEARL FROM GOD

"Therefore encourage one another and build each other up, just as in fact you are doing." (1 Thessalonians 5:11)

A PRINCIPLE TO LIVE BY

Be an encourager, beloved. Build others up with kind words and your support.

Chapter 3:
Willow Springs

"They will spring up like grass in a meadow, like willow trees by flowing streams." (Isaiah 44:4)

After the Pledge of Allegiance to the flag, Mrs. Robinson opened a King James Bible. *"In the beginning God created the heaven and the earth,"* she read. *"And the earth was without form, and void; and darkness was upon the face of the deep. And the Spirit of God moved upon the face of the waters. And God said, 'Let there be light;' and there was light."*

Every morning of fifth grade that year would begin with the pledge, the Bible, and a prayer.

Mrs. Robinson held up a stack of papers. "Children, you have twenty minutes to answer these fifty fill-in-the-blank questions."

A groan crossed the room.

"This isn't a test, knuckleheads. There are no right or wrong answers. It's just a way of getting to know each other. Write whatever comes to your mind, and afterwards, you can share only if you want to."

She handed out the sheets printed in purple ink fresh off the mimeograph machine in the principal's office. (A mimeograph machine was a printing contraption that worked by forcing ink through a stencil onto paper, and all the teachers in the whole school had to share just one, measly machine.)

I read the first question: *"My greatest fear is"* and filled in the blank with <u>thinking of my family dying</u>.

#2. I try hard <u>to be likable</u>.

#3. If I would only <u>try, I would learn to ride my unicycle.</u>

#4. Nothing is so frustrating as <u>getting in trouble for things you didn't do.</u>

#5. It is embarrassing <u>to have something told in front of you that you did wrong.</u>

#6. The meanest thing I ever did <u>was kick Mark while he wasn't looking.</u>

#7. People think of me <u>as a tomboy.</u>

#8. My worst fault is <u>talking too much.</u>

#9. There are times <u>when I have to get away and just sit alone.</u>

#10. At night <u>I'm sometimes scared.</u>

With four and a half minutes to spare, I wrote my last answer: #50. If I had 3 wishes, they would be <u>I wish the world had peace, I wish I had a horse, and I wish I had 100 more wishes</u>. When Mrs. Robinson asked who wanted to share their answers, I was first to raise my hand.

After lunch, Mrs. Robinson asked Runae to hand out *The Weekly Readers*, a children's newspaper which began in 1928 as *My Weekly Reader*. "Moon Suits Will Protect Spacemen" marked today's headlines.

I raised a hand.

"Yes, Jill."

"Mrs. Robinson, do you think we'll ever get a man on the moon?"

"I do. You children may not remember, but back in 1961, President Kennedy called a special joint session of Congress and challenged our nation to land a man on the moon before the decade ends, and NASA is making great strides toward that goal. Now, who wants to read first?"

My hand shot up, but Mrs. Robinson called on Lisa. She read, "*Scientists have made a strange-looking space suit. Someday, a man may wear such a suit on the moon. A man from earth cannot live on the moon without a special kind of suit. There is no air on the moon."*

The best part of the day was recess. Our class shared the playground with Mrs. Wilson's. The boys ran straight to the baseball field, and the two captains appointed by the teachers choose teammates. The girls scattered to the swings, merry-go-round, monkey bars, and seesaws. I picked up a braided rope and jumped to: "Cinderella, dressed in yellow, went upstairs to see her fellow. "

"Hey, look what I found," Nina Boyce called.

I dropped the rope and joined the girls crowded around my friend holding a rosebud-shaped rock.

"What is it?" Karen asked.

"A fossil," Nina Boyce answered. She pulled a tiny stone marked with rings from her pocket. "And I think this one's a petrified fish bone. They're all over the place out here."

I searched the ground. "Here's one." I picked up a stone bone and handed it to her. "Hey, Karen, race you to the top of the monkey bars. Ready, set, go!"

Karen was off like a shot. We ran as hard as we could and scrambled up the metal bars, giggling and slapping the top at the same time.

"Tie!" Karen shouted.

I gasped for air. "I wish . . . I wish we were in the same class this year."

Karen panted. "Yeah . . . me, too . . . But at least we have recess together."

"Yeah."

Karen tugged a sock. "What'd ya do this summer?"

"Uh, swimming lessons and Bible school and Mark and I spent a week with our grandmother in Florence, Alabama. Our cousins from Michigan came, too. What about you?"

"We swam every day at our new house. Well, it's not really new. It's an old house — fifty years old — but it's new to us."

"Where is it?"

"Out on Highway 11 like you're going to Valley Head. You know that white house with columns up on the hill before you get to Mary Igou's house?"

My eyes bugged. "You mean that huge *mansion?* The one my daddy calls the old Snodgrass Place?"

Karen laughed. "That's the one."

"WOW!!!"

"We love it. There are pastures and woods and a spring that pumps gallons and gallons of water. Daddy says it could supply all of Fort Payne if need be."

Karen's daddy was Dr. Charles Isbell. Their family had moved to Fort Payne the year before, and Karen and I had become friends as fourth graders in Mrs. Green's class at Forest Avenue School.

"Our place is called Willow Springs 'cause there are so many willow trees beside the stream. One's so big it was named the Alabama state champion willow tree last year."

"Willow Springs? I love that name. It sounds so . . . I don't know . . . It sounds . . ."

"Magical?"

"Yeah, magical."

REFLECTIONS

A POINT TO PONDER

What grew by the spring at the Isbell's new homeplace? In the Bible, God often used *trees* to represent flourishing people.

A PEARL FROM GOD

"Blessed is the one . . . whose delight is in the law of the Lord and meditates on His law day and night. That person is like a tree planted by streams of water, which yields its fruit in season and whose leaf does not wither — whatever they do prospers." (Psalm 1:1-3)

A PRINCIPLE TO LIVE BY

God's promise: life is better, healthier, and stronger for people who read, love, and obey the Word of God. Read God's Word every day, beloved.

Chapter 4:

The Boat Club

"The next day we set sail . . ." (Acts 20:15)

"Pull the rope a little tighter," Daddy told Mark after school on Thursday. Mark tugged. Daddy tied a clove-hitch knot, securing the mast and boom.

Our daddy enjoyed taking the sailboat to the Boat Club on his days off. Like most businessmen in Fort Payne, he closed shop Thursday and Saturday afternoons (and all day Sundays, of course).

He checked the trailer hitch a second time. "Better hurry, kids. Now that school's started back, we don't have long."

The Fort Payne Boat Club was a far cry from those highfalutin' yacht clubs where men dress in blue blazers and ladies sip mint iced tea. Our club — a boat ramp, three wooden docks, and a concrete-block bathhouse in the middle of a pasture — sat on the bank of the Tennessee River near Scottsboro and was the ideal place to sail the little dinghy that Daddy and Mark had built in our garage.

On Monday, just four days prior, our family had been at the club for the annual Labor Day picnic. Daddy's job this year was picking up a mountain of Mud Creek barbeque to feed thirty families. All of us but Rocky (a senior in high school) rode over in the Ford. Daddy had let him drive the green and white 1960 Willis jeep since he brought a girlfriend.

Today, Rocky stayed after school to practice basketball even though the season didn't start till November. Our big brother had always preferred sports to water.

Mama stepped out on the front porch and waved. "Y'all have fun."

I hollered out the window, "Don't you wanna come with us, Mama?"

"No, thanks. I need to catch up on things around the house and cook supper."

Daddy pushed in an eight-track tape. The whole thirty-eight-minute ride to the river, he tapped his foot to "The Yellow Rose of Texas," "When the Blue of the

Night Meets the Gold of the Day," Pete Fountain's "Just a Closer Walk with Thee," and Herb Alpert and The Tijuana Brass' rendition of "Spanish Flea."

Down Lookout Mountain.

Across the valley.

Over Pine Ridge.

Up Sand Mountain.

Across the flat top.

Past the newly built Northeast State Community College.

Down the west side of Sand Mountain.

The view never lost its charm. Southern pines stood tall between Highway 35 and the overlook. Under the bluff, the broad Tennessee River spread across the valley. Tree-covered islands speckled the sparkling waterway.

I read a rusty sign nailed to a pine tree, "The Evening Star Drive Inn Café. Outside Tables. Clean Restrooms. Hey, Daddy, we should eat there sometime."

"There's the bridge." Mark pointed to the steel, two-lane B. B. Comer Bridge stretching 2,143 feet over the Tennessee River.

On the other side of the river, a restaurant sat beside the highway. Its red-stained siding matched red-checkered curtains in the windows. "There's Freck's Café," I said. "We're almost there."

Just past the restaurant, Daddy turned left at the Fort Payne Boat Club sign and followed the narrow road to the gate. He studied the sky. "Clear, seventy-eight degrees, and a stiff breeze — perfect sailing weather."

"Duck your head, Jill."

I ducked just as the boom, a wooden pole along the foot of the white-cloth sail, swung over the boat. The mainsail (and only sail) fluttered in the breeze and then snapped tight. The dinghy cut through the water like a hot knife through butter.

Mark and I shared the front bench. Daddy sat in the stern with a hand on the tiller, the wooden stick attached to the rudder that steered the vessel. "You wanna steer, Mark?"

His face lit up. "Yes, sir!"

Daddy moved to the bench next to me. He patted my knee but kept an eye on Mark. "So, Mark, how are you and Mr. McKay getting along now?"

"A little better." The sail wrinkled. Mark adjusted the tiller to catch the wind. "Yesterday, I stayed after class and cleaned the chalkboard and erasers. He seemed to appreciate it. And I found out that Mr. McKay likes sailboats, too. That gave us something to talk about."

"Good."

Water lapped the hull. My fingertips trailed through the river. "Daddy, did you ever get in trouble when you were a kid?"

He laughed, his shoulders shaking up and down. "I did. More times than I care to remember."

"What did you do wrong?" Mark asked.

"Mostly talked too much."

My head bobbed. "Me, too!"

Daddy grinned. "Talked too much and argued. My teachers said I could argue with a fence post."

"Well, I guess that's why you're a good lawyer," Mark said.

Daddy chuckled. "Maybe so."

We circled a small island. A crow left a pine branch with a loud CAW, CAW. Mark squawked back. A motorboat cut through the river, pushing out waves. The dinghy rocked to and fro.

"Turn perpendicular, Mark," Daddy said. "If you run parallel to the waves, we might tip over."

Mark turned.

"Good."

We headed to the next island.

"Hey, Daddy," Mark said, "there's a new show coming on NBC tonight. If we finish all our homework, can we watch it?"

"What is it?"

"Star Trek. It's about outer space. Everybody's talking about it at school."

"Is it in color?" I asked.

Mark shrugged. "I don't know. We'll have to watch for the peacock."

Starting in 1956, the year I was born, NBC's peacock logo would magically transform from black and white to a rainbow of colors before every program broadcasted in living color. Although more and more shows were moving to full color on the three networks (NBC, CBS, and ABC), the changing peacock still thrilled our family since the only color TV we'd ever owned was less than a year old.

"If y'all get your homework done, maybe we can watch it together."

"Mark, will you call out my spelling words on the way home? I have a test tomorrow."

"Sure."

An hour later, Daddy glanced at his watch. "Well, time flies when you're having fun. Mark, you better take us to the dock. By the time we get to shore, load the boat, and drive home, your mama will have supper on the table."

"What are we having?" Mark asked.

"Meatloaf, black-eyed peas, creamed potatoes, and your mama's good buttermilk biscuits."

My mouth watered. "Oh boy! I'm starving."

As we sailed toward the Boat Club, Daddy picked up my hand and studied it. "Your mama used to have pretty hands like this until you kids worked 'em to the bone."

I liked Daddy holding my hand. I liked him calling it pretty.

REFLECTIONS

A POINT TO PONDER

What got my daddy, Mark, and me in trouble at school?

A PEARL FROM GOD

"My dear brothers and sisters, take note of this: Everyone should be quick to listen, slow to speak and slow to become angry." (James 1:19) "A truly wise person uses few words; a person with understanding is even-tempered." (Proverbs 17:27 NLT)

A PRINCIPLE TO LIVE BY

God gave us two ears and one mouth. Beloved, practice listening twice as much as you talk and think before you speak.

Chapter 5:
The Window

". . . There he stands behind our wall,
gazing through the window,
peering through the lattice."
(Song of Solomon 2:9)

"What's she saying? What's she saying?" I begged.

Mama put a finger to her lips. "That sounds nice, Barbara. She'll be excited."

I strained toward the telephone receiver.

"Okay. See you around nine on Saturday. Thank you. Bye, now." She hung up smiling. "Mrs. Isbell invited you to come to their house Saturday. Is that okay?"

"Yes, ma'am!" I jumped in circles chanting, "I'm going to Wil-low-Spr-ings! I'm going to Wil-low-Spr-ings!"

September had bid farewell, and October arrived in a ray of glory. Splashes of yellow and red painted the mountainsides and valley. A giant sugar maple on the corner of 5th Street and Godfrey Avenue had turned from green, to gold, to a blaze of fiery orange. "That's my favorite tree in the whole town," Mama would say every fall.

On Saturday, we drove up the winding driveway bordered by a whitewashed fence.

I gawked at the big house. "Karen lives in a mansion!"

Mama nodded. "It's pretty, isn't it?"

Under the blue sky, the stately manor topped a rolling hill. Stones covered the retaining walls, foundation, and twelve front steps. (I counted from the car.) Black shutters edged windows on the first and second stories, and four massive columns with scrolled tops (Mama called them Greek Ionic) lined the portico. A lantern-like chandelier hung by a chain from the high porch ceiling, and the red front door looked freshly painted. Brick chimneys rose from the gray roof — one on each end of the house.

Karen stood on the driveway waving. "Hurry, Jill! I have so much to show you."

"Bye, Mama. See ya this afternoon." I pecked her cheek with a kiss and clambered out of the car.

Karen grabbed my arm. "Let's go to the meadow. I wanna show you the spring. Race you!"

Mama called after me. "Jill, you behave yourself."

"Yes, ma'am," I hollered back.

At the bottom of the hill, Karen said, "Tada! Here it is!"

Crystal water bubbled from the ground and flowed down a meandering stream. Willows trees stood on both sides like soldiers on guard. She pointed to the water's edge. "See that green stuff? It's watercress. Laura and Chuck and I picked some yesterday, and Mama made watercress sandwiches."

Laura and Chuck were Karen's little sister and brother. Laura was in the first grade at Forest Avenue. Chuck was only four (the same age as my cousin, Vicki) and hadn't started school yet.

"Does it taste good?"

"Yeah. Here, try some." She handed me a sprig.

I chewed the round, green leaves. "It's kinda peppery." I stuck my hand in the chilly water. "How much water did your daddy say comes out of here?"

"Over a million gallons a day, and it's 55 degrees all year-round. One night a long time ago, my great-granddaddy, John B. Isbell, Sr., camped under an oak tree close to this spring when he was driving cattle from Martling in Marshall County to Chattanooga."

"Hey, look, I'm a cow!" I said and bent over, pretending to drink from the stream.

Karen laughed. "Me, too!" she said and stuck her face in the water. She splashed me. I giggled and splashed back.

"Come on." She motioned for me to follow. "You gotta see where the little house used to be."

"What little house?"

"Maude Pendergrass's little house. She lived there when the two sisters built the big house in 1916. Maude called it the mansion."

Karen grinned when I said, "I told Mama you lived in a mansion."

We wandered around a pasture dotted with black-eyed Susans. A thicket of woods stood behind the field that reminded me of my granddaddy's farm on top of Lookout Mountain.

I picked a yellow, daisy-like flower. "Did you know black-eyed Susans are in the sunflower family?"

"Really? I love sunflowers."

"That's what Grandmama Nance told me. She loves flowers, too. Her favorites are the wild, purple violets that bloom in the springtime."

"Mrs. Bethune — that's the family who owned Willow Springs before us — told me that next spring a row of daffodils will bloom right here where the yard of the little house used to be. She said they come up every year."

"I wonder what that little house looked like." I tucked a flower behind my ear and stuck out my hand. "Howdy-do, ma'am, my name's Maude. Would you like to come set a spell on my front porch?"

Karen shook my hand vigorously. "Why, thank ya, kindly, good neighbor. I shorely would. Right nice weather we've been having, ain't it?"

"Bluest sky I ever did see. Reminds me of my girlhood back on the farm."

We collapsed in the grass laughing. Karen said, "Wanna see our house now?"

"Sure! Race you up the hill."

"Tie!" she yelled when our tennis shoes slapped the step-stone walkway at the same time.

"Did you say two *sisters* built your house?"

"Yeah, the Thomason sisters, Mrs. Eliza Thomason Snodgrass and Mrs. Leona Thomason Davis. They built it as a memorial to their parents, John and Mary Elizabeth Thomason."

"How come you know so much about Willow Springs?"

"'Cause Mama and Daddy studied its history before we bought it." She pointed to the right end of the house and put on a prim-and-proper face. "So, Miss Maude, over there is our big sunporch overlooking the pool."

I gasped. "You have a pool, Mrs. Snodgrass? Well, I declare!"

"And up there on the second floor, that first window is my room, and the next one is the bathroom, and that little window is... that's the . . . that's . . . uh . . . hmm. You know, I don't remember a little window upstairs. Come on. Let's go see."

We dashed up the stone steps, across the porch, and through the red front door. Inside, an elegant chandelier hung from the ceiling over polished, hardwood floors. A huge brick fireplace (one of nine in the house) with a wide, white mantle sat on one end of the rectangular living room, and glass French doors that led to a small den stood on the opposite end. Two large openings led to a spacious dining room and a central hallway where we found the stairs. I raced Karen up the hardwood staircase with dark handrails and carved, wooden spindles.

"This is my room."

I peeked in. A white coverlet sprinkled with lavender violets lay across her double bed. Eyelet curtains covered the bottom half of the tall window facing Lookout Mountain, and a matching valance fringed the top.

"You have a grand view of the mountain," I told Karen, but she was already on to the next room.

"And here's the bathroom with one window." She pulled back a teal-blue shower curtain. "Nope. No little window in here." She dashed into the hallway. "And here are the bookshelves and the hall window. And here's Laura's room. She has one big window, just like me. That makes one, two, three, four . . . but where's that little window we saw from out front — the fifth one? Let's go count again."

We studied the house from the front yard.

Karen recounted. "One, two, three, four, five. Okay, that's my window, and there's the bathroom window. There's the window we couldn't find. There's the hall window and Laura's window. Four inside and five outside, right?"

"Yep, I see five."

"That's weird."

"Really weird." I stared at the middle window. "So, we can see it from out here . . . but we can't see it when we're in the house. And if we can't see it from inside, that means your house has . . . "

We looked at each other and exclaimed together, "A secret room!"

"Come on, Jill. We gotta tell Mama!"

REFLECTIONS

A POINT TO PONDER

What did Karen discover? Did you know that the Bible speaks of the "secret place" of God?

A PEARL FROM GOD

"He that dwelleth in the secret place of the Most High shall abide under the shadow of the Almighty. I will say of the LORD, He is my refuge and my fortress: my God; in Him I will trust." (Psalm 91:1-2 KJV)

A PRINCIPLE TO LIVE BY

The "secret place of God" is not a physical location but rather our relationship with Him. Those who live in close communion with God are sheltered under His protection in good times and hard times. Beloved, stay close to God and always trust in Him.

Chapter 6:

A Hunting We Will Go

"He was the greatest hunter in the world..."
(Genesis 10:9 NLT)

Rocky, Mark, and I never considered the hard work it took to go to Sunday School and church on a Sunday morning and get a delicious dinner fit for a king on the table by twelve forty-five. But, somehow, Mama managed it every week with little help from us. (I would set the table when she asked me to, and Daddy had trained us kids to take our dirty dishes to the sink when we were done.)

"Aren ound a ecre oom," I mumbled at the Sunday lunch table.

Mama patted my arm. "Jill, don't talk with your mouth full."

I swallowed a bite of drumstick and turned the lazy-Susan to help myself to more fried okra. "I said Karen found a secret room in her new house."

47

Rocky reached for a biscuit. "What's in the room?"

"Don't know. There's not a door. Just a little window on the second floor that we could see from the yard, but we couldn't find it inside the house."

"Did you get a ladder and look in the window?" Mark asked.

"Nope, too high. Besides, Dr. Isbell wouldn't let us."

Mark looked thoughtful. "I wonder what's in there. And why would there be a room without a door? Jill, the next time you go to Karen's, ask her if I can go, too."

"Okay."

Rocky added two drops of Sweeta to his tea and said, "The fourth game of the World Series is this afternoon."

The World Series didn't matter a hill of beans to me, but I tried to act interested. "Who's playing?"

"Baltimore Orioles and the Los Angeles Dodgers."

"I hope the Oreos win."

Daddy grinned. "Why, sugar?"

"'Cause I like cookies better than cars and trucks."

My brothers burst out laughing. I could tell Daddy and Mama were trying not to.

I shrugged. "What?"

Rocky explained, "It's *Orioles* not Oreos, silly girl. And it's the *Dodgers,* not Dodge like the car manufacturer. The LA Dodgers used to be the Brooklyn Trolley Dodgers who got their name from New York people *dodging* trolleys to keep from getting run over. Later they shortened the name to just Dodgers."

"Oh, okay. Well, I still pick the Oreos. Can I have a cookie?"

I was disappointed when the next week of reading and writing and 'rithmetic ended without another invitation to Willow Springs, but Daddy told Mark and me that we could go quail hunting with him at Dan Walker's farm on Saturday if we got up in time.

We did.

Rocky didn't hunt much anymore. Sports, school, a girlfriend, and a job occupied his time. When he turned sixteen, our neighbor, Mr. Raymond, had hired him as a guide at Manitou Cave for 85¢ an hour.

The Raymond family had owned the cave and surrounding property since the early 1900s. A few years ago, they had opened it as a tourist attraction and had also stocked it with non-perishable canned goods, blankets, and other life-sustaining supplies to serve as a fallout shelter where people could live in case of nuclear war.

At school, we had "duck and cover" air-raid drills should the Soviet Union ever bomb the United States. The teachers had us crawl under desks and cover our heads. Every drill, I envisioned bombs blowing up the school and wanted to run home and hide. I prayed hard that my family would never have to live in a cave.

The Willis jeep chugged past Eberhart's grocery at Five Points on the top of the mountain and continued down Adamsburg Road. I sat on the front seat between Mark and Daddy, and our hunting dog, Rip, stood behind him with his front paws on Daddy's shoulders. Rip howled; Daddy sang:

"Takes a rocking chair to rock,
Takes a rubber ball to roll,
Takes a red-headed woman
To satisfy my soul."

(Not one of Mama's favorite jingles.)

Near the farm, Mark nodded toward a two-story, abandoned house. "There's the old Carbide place."

The house with boarded windows looked sad and lonesome under tall oak trees. I wondered where its family had gone and why it stood empty now. In my mind, I rewrote its story and imagined cheerful children playing in the tall weeds.

When we got to Mr. Walker's farm, he was waiting with his dog, Joe. Daddy let Rip out of the jeep. He darted straight to Joe, and they ran laps around the yard.

I laughed. "Look, they're doing a happy dance."

Mark and I followed the men and dogs to a cornfield behind the farmhouse. Daddy handed me his leather cap. Mark and I filled it with popcorn ears from the dry stalks. The men sent Rip and Joe on ahead with a loud, "Go find 'em!"

51

Hunting trips with Daddy and Mr. Walker were more walking and talking than shooting. Mark and I enjoyed listening to their hunting tales and World War II stories.

Daddy had gone overseas aboard a warship that passed under the Golden Gate Bridge. The ship's commander stood on the bow with big tears rolling down his cheeks. Over two years later, Daddy rode home in a transport plane that flew over that same bridge. He told Mr. Walker, "I've been over the Golden Gate and under it but never on it." I was surprised what I learned by listening more and talking less.

At a cotton field an hour later, Rip froze — nose forward, front paw raised, tail as straight as an arrow.

"Look, Rip's got something," I whispered.

Mark put his finger to his lips.

"Hold," Daddy commanded softly. "Hold."

He crept up beside the stone-still dog, raised a 12-gauge shotgun, and hollered, "Flush!"

Rip leaped; a large covey of quail took flight.

BANG!

BANG!

BANG! BANG!

"Fetch!"

Rip retrieved and dropped two birds at Daddy's feet. Joe brought one to Mr. Walker.

Daddy patted the square, brown head. "Good boy. That's a good boy, Rip."

At noon, Daddy tuned the small transistor radio in his vest pocket to 1400 WFPA, our local station. The Alabama/Tennessee football game from Neyland Stadium in Knoxville was on.

Mr. Walker grinned when he heard the radio. "Oh, you've got one of them music boxes."

Last year had been a banner season for Coach Bear Bryant and the Crimson Tide, ending in a 9-1-1 record. Their victory over Nebraska in the Orange Bowl had earned them the title of 1965 National Champions in the AP Poll. This year, Bama was undefeated with victories over Louisiana Tech, Old Miss, and Clemson.

Midafternoon, at the beginning of the fourth quarter, we hiked back to the jeep. Daddy and Mr. Walker's pockets bulged with birds.

No fried chicken on the menu tomorrow, I thought. *We're having quail for Sunday lunch.*

When the man on the radio announced that Alabama trailed the Volunteers 10-0, Daddy shook his head. "I don't know if the Bear can pull this one out of the hole. Clock's ticking."

Well, we don't know what Coach Bryant told those boys during a timeout, but by some miracle (I think my friend Mary was praying), the team rallied and pulled ahead with an 11-10 lead. But in the final minute of play, Tennessee marched into field goal range.

"The snap is good," Alabama's John Forney announced. "Good catch, good hold, and the kick is . . . the kick is . . . NO GOOD!!!" he screamed. "NO GOOD! Tennessee misses the game-winning field goal! The

Alabama Crimson Tide has defeated the Tennessee Volunteers 11-10 and remains unbeaten! The Bama crowd is going wild."

Daddy hollered, "Roll Tide!"

Mr. Walker grinned.

I turned a cartwheel.

Mark didn't do anything. He'd rather play football than listen to it.

Back at the jeep, Daddy found a sack of walnuts sitting on the front seat — a small but kind gift left by Mr. Walker's daddy.

On the way home, I pulled a wrinkly, brown shell from the sack and hit it hard against the metal window frame. It didn't even crack. I studied the walnut in the palm of my hand. *If I were an ant*, I thought, *I could hide inside a walnut shell.* Out loud, I chanted, "Peter, Peter pumpkin eater, had a wife and couldn't keep her. Put her in a pumpkin shell. There he kept her very well."

REFLECTIONS

A POINT TO PONDER

As a little puppy, do you think Rip knew how to hunt, point, flush, and retrieve? Of course not. Daddy had to _____ him.

A PEARL FROM GOD

"No discipline seems pleasant at the time, but painful. Later on, however, it produces a harvest of righteousness and peace for those who have been trained by it. Therefore, strengthen your feeble arms and weak knees." (Hebrews 12:11-12)

A PRINCIPLE TO LIVE BY

When life is hard, beloved, view your circumstance as an opportunity for God to train you. If you listen to, learn from, and obey Him, you'll become a strong and skilled man or woman of God.

Chapter 7:
Fort McKay

"The LORD is my rock, my fortress and my deliverer; my
God is my rock in whom I take refuge, my shield
and the horn of my salvation,
my stronghold." (Psalm 18:2)

After school on Thursday, I found Daddy and Mark on the screened-in porch. A sheet of plywood balanced across the rock picnic table. Daddy was staining it brown, and Mark was gluing popsicle sticks to a wooden block shaped like a cabin.

"Whatcha making?"

Mark picked up another stick and smeared Elmer's wood glue on the back. "A fort."

"How come?"

"'Cause we're studying the Civil War in American history, and Mr. McKay assigned a special project. We gotta make something related to the War Between the States and then give a report in front of the whole class. I'm making a fort. I'm gonna name it Fort McKay."

"Why didn't you name it Fort Payne?"

"'Cause the fort in Fort Payne wasn't part of the Civil War. Besides, it wasn't really a fort. It was a stockade built to hold Cherokees forced to leave their homes and walk the Trail of Tears. I think it was only used for about a year." Mark's face grew serious. "That's sad to me. The purpose of a fort is to keep people safe. Fort Payne kept people prisoners."

I imagined getting ripped from my home and locked up. "That *is* sad. It's awful! We studied the Trail of Tears in Alabama history when I was in Mrs. Hixon's third grade class."

"Yeah, I had Mrs. Kuykendall in third grade. She made us do a 'Trail of Tears' coloring sheet. I hated coloring sheets."

"Why do you think they did it?"

"Did what? Make us do coloring sheets?"

"No, silly-willy, why did the government make the Cherokees leave their homes?"

"'Cause men do awful things sometimes."

Daddy dipped the paintbrush into the can of cherrywood stain. He didn't say anything, but I could tell he was listening.

"Mr. McKay said that when gold was discovered near Dahlonega, Georgia, they passed the Indian Removal Act and forced thousands of Native Americans to leave their homelands and move west of the Mississippi River. So, I guess greed was why."

"So, does Mr. McKay like you now?"

"I think so. Maybe he'll like me even better when he sees Fort McKay. It's gonna be the best project in the eighth grade thanks to Daddy."

Daddy smiled and kept painting.

REFLECTIONS

A POINT TO PONDER

Mark said that the purpose of a fort is to keep people _____.

A PEARL FROM GOD

"The name of the LORD is a fortified tower; the righteous run to it and are safe." (Proverbs 18:10)

A PRINCIPLE TO LIVE BY

Television personality Mister Fred Rogers once told children, "If you are in danger, always look for the helpers." And I would add, "If you are in danger, beloved, always call out to Jesus. He is your fortress, strength, and a very present Helper in times of trouble."

Chapter 8:

Into the Darkness

"I will give thee the treasures of darkness and hidden riches of secret places..."
(Isaiah 45:3 KJV)

The following Friday, Karen found me on the playground. "Guess what, Jill! Guess what!"

"What?"

"Daddy borrowed an extension ladder from a carpenter that's working on our house and . . ."

"Mr. Robinson? Jack Robinson? I know him! Not Mrs. Robinson's Mr. Robinson. Another Mr. Robinson. He screened in our back porch, and me and Mark and Freddy and Steve used to sit on the rock table while he worked and tell stories. Mr. Robinson — the carpenter Mr. Robinson not my teacher's Mr. Robinson — liked to listen. One time . . ."

Karen grabbed my arm. She looked like she was about to explode. "Listen to me, Jill! Daddy climbed the ladder to the little window yesterday!"

My mouth flew open. "Well, why didn't you say so in the first place? What'd he find?"

"Nothing 'cause it's stuck, and there's a curtain blocking the view. But even if he could've opened it, he's too big to get through."

"My brother Mark's a good climber. I bet he could fit through that window."

"That's a great idea!"

"And Mark already said he wants to come to your house sometime. Hey, I know. Ask your Daddy if we can come over tomorrow."

"Sounds like a plan!" We shook on it.

Mama eyed the tall ladder on the Isbell's front porch as we pulled up the driveway. "Winfred, that's awfully high. Do you think it's safe?"

Mark leaned over the front seat. "Mama, I'll be fine. It's not as tall as the trees we climb."

She nodded. "True but be careful."

"Yes, ma'am, I will."

The entire Isbell family came out to greet us. The grown folks exchanged pleasantries. Chuck instantly took to Mark and showed him how fast he could run.

Mark squatted to his level. "Wow! You're faster than the roadrunner."

Mrs. Isbell laughed. "Oh, you've made his day, Mark. That's his favorite cartoon. Chuck loves the roadrunner. Don't you, honey?"

"Beep, beep," he twittered and circled the yard again.

Daddy asked Dr. Isbell, "Were you listening to the game? Looks like Alabama's gonna be 5-0 this week. They're killing Vanderbilt."

Mama leaned toward Mrs. Isbell. "Mark and Jill can't stop talking about this mysterious room Karen found."

She laughed. "Oh, I know what you mean. Our kids have about driven Charles crazy trying to figure out a way to get inside."

"Charles, what did you have in mind?" Daddy held out a toolbox. "I brought tools. I could climb up first and try to unjam the window."

Dr. Isabell nodded. "Sounds good to me. But it could be locked on the inside, you know."

"Yeah, I thought of that, too. Hopefully, it's just painted shut. I brought a putty knife to cut the seal."

Dr. Isbell held the ladder steady. Daddy climbed to the second story. He pulled the putty knife from a pocket, pushed it in between the window sash and the frame, and then worked around the window.

Dr. Isbell watched. "Now try it, Winfred."

Daddy pushed. "Nope. Jiggled a little, but still won't open. I'll try the hammer."

I gasped. "Hammer? Mama, is Daddy gonna smash the window?"

She smiled. "Just watch and see."

Daddy tap, tap, tapped across the bottom, top, and both sides. "Here goes!"

He shoved.

Nothing.

Karen stomped her foot. "Awe, man!"

Mama studied the window. "Hey, Winfred, I just had a thought. Maybe it's one of those old casement windows that swings in and out like a door instead of sliding up and down."

"How does your mother know about that?" Karen whispered.

"She's a librarian. She knows all kinds of stuff 'cause she reads *all* the time."

Daddy stuck the knife in the right side and pried. "It moved!"

Karen and I jumped up and down. Laura watched and jumped up and down, too.

"It's coming!"

One more pry and the window sprung open. He pushed back the threadbare curtain and waved dust from the air. "Charles (cough), Mark's gonna need a good flashlight."

"I'll get one, Winfred."

Mrs. Isbell soon returned with an Eveready Captain 6-volt lantern.

Daddy climbed down. Mark climbed up and disappeared into the darkness.

REFLECTIONS

A POINT TO PONDER

When Mama offered a suggestion, did Daddy listen?

A PEARL FROM GOD

"Fools think their own way is right, but the wise listen to others." (Proverbs 12:15 NLT)

A PRINCIPLE TO LIVE BY

Don't ever think you know it all, beloved. Be wise. Listen to good advice from your family, friends, teachers, and, most importantly, the all-knowing, all-wise Lord God Almighty.

Chapter 9:

The Secret Room

"For all that is secret will eventually be brought into the open, and everything that is concealed will be brought to light and made known to all." (Luke 8:17 NLT)

All eyes glued to the little window. Out of the darkness came a loud "Wow!"

"What is it, Mark?" I yelled.

Karen cupped her hands around her mouth. "What'd ya find?"

He poked his head out. "It's really neat!" And then vanished again.

"What's neat?" Laura peeped.

"Found a switch." Light and Mark filled the window. "Y'all gotta see this. Can Jill and Karen come up?"

I dropped to my knees with my hands clasped together. "Please, please, please, Daddy? I can do it. I've been climbing trees since I was three. I'll be careful. I promise."

"Please, Daddy?" Karen begged. "After all, I'm the one who found the room."

Our daddies looked at each other. My daddy shrugged. "Fine with me."

Dr. Isbell nodded. "Okay."

"Girls, you be careful," Mrs. Isbell said.

Mama added, "Watch your step."

I ran to the ladder but stopped. "It's your house, Karen. You go first."

"Thanks!"

She scaled the rungs. I stayed right on her heels. "Just like a couple of monkeys," I heard Daddy say as we piled through the window.

The tiny room held a small, wooden desk and seven chairs crammed in a circle. Bookshelves lined with dusty books and cobwebs filled the back and right-hand walls. The left wall, however, made our jaws drop. From plank floor to ceiling, a breathtaking painting of willow trees beside a bubbling brook covered the entire wall. Hand-scripted letters across the top read: *As Willows by the Water Courses, O Jesurun.*

I took in every detail — the blue sky with wispy, white clouds. Delicate, jade leaves on thin, weepy branches. A bright-red cardinal in flight.

Tall grass laced with yellow wildflowers. A rushing stream patched with green watercress.

"Karen, this is your spring down in the meadow! The one you showed me."

"I know!" She read the odd message capping the painting, "As willows by the water courses, O Je . . . Jesu . . . Jesurun. What in the world does that mean?"

I shrugged. "Who is Jesurun?"

Mark picked a book up from the desk and wiped the dust with his shirttail. "A 1930 Boy Scout Handbook. You think the Boy Scouts met up here?"

I wagged my head. "Nah, I think it was a *secret* club. Maybe the books will give us a clue."

He ran a finger across the volumes. "Here's a set of 1919 World Book Encyclopedias and an old King James Bible. *The Hobbit* by J.R.R. Tolkien, and *National Velvet* by Enid Bagnold, and *Call of the Wild* by Jack London. That's one of the best books I ever read. Here's *Robinson Crusoe* by Daniel Defoe. It's a library of old classics."

I read titles over Mark's shoulder. "Wait till Mama hears about this!"

Karen's eyes never left the painting. "Look! There's a name and date in the bottom corner."

I leaned down. "It says James Ralph Johnson, October 8, 1939."

REFLECTIONS

A POINT TO PONDER

Who was the artist that painted the beautiful landscape in the secret room?

A PEARL FROM GOD

"For we are God's masterpiece. He has created us anew in Christ Jesus, so we can do the good things He planned for us long ago." (Ephesians 2:10 NLT)

A PRINCIPLE TO LIVE BY

Beloved, you are a work of art — God's masterpiece. He made you and knit you together in a marvelous and wonderful way. He knows everything about you and loves you just the way you are. Always put your hope and trust in Him.

Chapter 10:

James Ralph Johnson

*"I have filled him with the Spirit of God in wisdom,
understanding, in knowledge, and in all kinds of skills —
to make artistic designs . . ."*
(Exodus 31:3-4)

We chattered from the window, "There's tons of books . . . And a huge painting . . . It's our spring and the willow trees . . . I found a Boy Scout Handbook from 1930."

"What? We can't understand a word you kids are saying." Dr. Isbell motioned. "Y'all come on down."

On the porch, Dr. Isbell said, "You go first, Mark."

"It's a tiny room, and there's a small desk . . ."

"Chairs are set up in a circle," I interrupted.

Daddy gave me "the look." I hushed.

Mark looked at Karen. "Tell 'em about the picture."

"Two walls are bookshelves stuffed with books, but one wall is a gigantic painting of our spring in the meadow."

I raised my hand. "And don't forget the weird words."

"You tell 'em, Jill."

"It said something about willows trees beside racehorses."

Mark cackled. "No, silly, it says as willows by the *water courses*, O Jesu . . . something."

"Jesurun!" Karen piped. "O, Jesurun."

"What, honey?" Mrs. Isbell asked.

"As willows by the water courses, O Jesurun."

"And at the bottom of the picture we found a name and date," I added.

"Yeah, James Ralph Johnson, October 8, 1939," Mark said.

Daddy's eyebrows raised. "James Ralph Johnson?"

"Yes, sir."

"I know him. He's Judge Andy Johnson's son and was a year behind me at DeKalb County High School."

Mrs. Isbell grabbed Chuck just before he flew off the porch like Underdog. "Winfred, maybe you could ask him about this mystery room in our house."

"Well, I haven't seen him in a while. I finished high school spring of '39. So, by that October, he was a senior, and I was a freshman at the University in Tuscaloosa."

"So, you haven't seen him since high school?"

"No, we've run into each other a few times over the years. I think he went to Howard College in Birmingham and then became an officer in the Marine Corp."

"Winfred, didn't he make the military his career?" Mama asked.

"Yes, he served in World War II and the Korean War, but somebody told me he's retired from the military now and lives in New Mexico. From what I understand, he's become a fairly successful author and artist."

Mama's face lit up. "You know, come think of it, he sent some information about his books to the Forest Avenue library a couple of years ago. He was still in the

Marines at that time and lived in Alexandria, Virginia. I know I kept the letter. I'll look for it Monday."

Pride swelled. *My daddy knows a famous author and artist!* I thought. *I sure hope Mama can find that letter.*

Mama picked us up from school Monday afternoon and handed me an envelope. "Found it! And look at the postmark."

"Marine Corps Schools Virginia, April 6, 1964. My eighth birthday!"

"Careful. Don't tear the papers."

"Here, Mark, you do it." I handed it to him.

Mark carefully unfolded two type-written pages — biographical information on both Mr. Johnson and his wife, Burdetta Fay Beebe Johnson (also a wildlife author) and a description of his books published by the David McKay Company in New York City. A third paper was in Mr. Johnson's own handwriting.

Mark read the biography aloud:

James Ralph Johnson was born in Fort Payne, Alabama. He served as field

scout executive for the Boy Scouts of America for seven years and has since been on active duty with the Marine Corps, serving in Iwo Jima, Japan, Korea, and Lebanon.

Upon his upcoming retirement from the Marine Corps in late 1964, Major and Mrs. Johnson plan to take a two-month camping trip to Alaska, and then settle permanently in Santa Fe, New Mexico. Though they will have a real house with a real roof as headquarters, they will live under the stars most of the time, making the Southwest area their perpetual camping grounds, and continuing their first-hand observations of animals and nature, so that they can fill many more books with fascinating data, stories, and illustrations for young people everywhere to enjoy.

I scooted closer to Mark. "What does the letter say?"

About twelve to fifteen years ago, I spent much time developing a book on the natural history of May's Gulf . . ."

"May's Gulf. Isn't that Little River Canyon?"

Mama nodded. "Yes, but just listen, Jill."

Mark started over:

About twelve to fifteen years ago, I spent much time developing a book on the natural history of May's Gulf, but unfortunately, like several subjects I've written about, the book was of much interest to me and of no interest to anyone else. So, the effort was never published.

One thing which always fascinated me about the gulf is the fact that May's

Gulf has today more native trees than all of Europe. I once listed well over eighty-five native species of trees found in the gulf. I also had a chapter on the green pitcher plant — one of the rarest plant species. (There are many pitcher plant species, but the green pitcher plant can be found only in DeKalb and Cherokee Counties and a small area in central Georgia.) My daughter and I found three locations where the plant grows along Little River. We examined the "stomachs" or traps of several and found a large grasshopper in one as well as the normal mass of dead flies and gnats.

Mama said, "Y'all want to run by the library and ask Mrs. Weatherly if she has a current address for the Johnsons?"

"Yes, ma'am!"

REFLECTIONS

A POINT TO PONDER

What rare plant did James Ralph Johnson and his daughter find along Little River in May's Gulf? A green _____ plant.

A PEARL FROM GOD

"*O LORD, what a variety of things You have made! In wisdom You have made them all. The earth is full of Your creatures.*" *(Psalm 104:24 NLT)*

A PRINCIPLE TO LIVE BY

Beloved, take a walk and find ten wonderful things that God created. Next, thank Him for His magnificent creation. (Did you put yourself on the list?)

Chapter 11:

Dear Mr. Johnson

"Write, therefore, what you have seen..."
(Revelation 1:19)

Dear Mr. Johnson,

My name is Jill Watson. I am in the fifth grade, and I live in Fort Payne, Alabama. My daddy is Winfred Watson. I think you went to school with him at DeKalb County High School. It's not DeKalb County High School anymore. It's Fort Payne High School now, and my brother Rocky is a senior there.

Last summer, my friend's family bought a gigantic old mansion on Highway 11. Her name is Karen Isbell. She found a little window on the second floor that you can see when you're outside, but you can't see it when you're inside. So, my brother Mark (he's in the eighth grade), Karen, and

I climbed up a ladder and crawled through the window. Don't worry, our parents said we could.

We found a secret room with lots of books. There's a giant painting on one wall that has your name in the corner. We have lots of questions. Here are our questions:

1. Did you paint that picture? It's really pretty.
2. Why is there a room without a door?
3. How did you get in the window?
4. What was the secret room used for?
5. Did Boy Scouts meet there?
6. Where did all the books come from?
7. What does "As the willows by the water courses, O Jesurun" mean?

We have more questions, but Mama said that seven is enough for now. I hope you get this letter. Please write back soon.

Sincerely,
Jill Watson

P.S. I forgot to tell you something. Mrs. Weatherly at the Dekalb Country Library gave us your address.

I stuffed the letter into an envelope, addressed it to James Ralph Johnson, Santa Fe, New Mexico, slapped on a 5¢ stamp, crossed my fingers, and said a prayer.

REFLECTIONS

A POINT TO PONDER

In my letter, how many questions did I ask Mr. Johnson? _____

A PEARL FROM GOD

"Call to Me and I will answer you and tell you great and unsearchable things you do not know." (Jeremiah 33:3)

A PRINCIPLE TO LIVE BY

Jeremiah 33:3 is sometimes called "God's phone number." Beloved, the Lord wants you to bring your questions to Him. Wisdom begins with God and wisdom belongs to God. He is eager to share His wisdom with you.

Chapter 12:

Open House

"Come and see..." (John 1:39 NLT)

At Williams Avenue School's Open House, I overheard Mrs. Robinson tell my parents, "One thing I'll say about Jill, she's enthusiastic. That girl raises her hand every time I ask a question and many times in between."

Is that a good thing or a bad thing, I wondered. *Daddy's smiling so it must be okay.*

Mark had insisted that Mama and Daddy visit my classroom first. "And save Mr. McKay's room for last," he said.

He must still be in trouble, I thought.

When Mrs. Robinson turned to speak to the next set of parents, Mama suggested that we head on over to the junior high to talk to Mark's teachers.

Daddy looked at Mark. "Okay, where to first, Mark?"

"Math class. Mrs. Lawrance.

"Lead the way."

Our parents had known Mrs. Isabell Lawrance for years. After their wedding on August 17, 1943, they had honeymooned at Summer Haven, a lovely cottage overlooking DeSoto Falls near Mentone, Alabama, owned by Mark's teacher and her mother, Mrs. Miller. Mama said she could remember an intricately carved windup music box at the cabin that played melodies by pins plucking a metal cylinder. Mrs. Lawrance told Mark that the valuable family heirloom had recently been stolen.

Her father, Arthur Abernathy Miller, was a well-known name around our town. In 1925, he had built a twenty-foot-high dam, named the A. A. Miller Dam,

above DeSoto Falls and a hydroelectric generator below the falls. It generated power for Fort Payne, Mentone,

Valley Head, and Collinsville, Alabama and Menlo, Georgia.

"Winfred and Verna, it's so good to see you." Mrs. Lawrance gave them a hug and nodded toward Mark. "You've done a good job with that one. He's such a helper and always kind to everyone."

In Mrs. Mac's science class, the periodic table chart hung next to the chalkboard and a life-sized human skeleton stood in one corner.

"What's that for?" I whispered.

Mark said, "We have to learn all 206 bones of the body."

Mrs. Mac looked at me and gave a half grin. "So, I see I have another Watson to look forward to. What grade are you in, honey?"

"Fifth."

"Mark, you and your sister better stay on your toes. Your brother, Rocky, set the bar pretty high. He's as smart as a whip."

We nodded. "Yes, ma'am."

In the gymnasium, Daddy talked to Coach Tucker, who just happened to be the brother-in-law of Mark's good friend, Eddy Everett. The coach ruffled Mark's hair. "Mark's as strong as an ox."

Mrs. Lands, the eighth-grade English teacher, told Mama that Mark was one of the sweetest students she had ever taught.

Well, all the teachers so far seem to like him, I thought.

I watched Mark's face as he guided us down the hallway toward the last stop: Mr. McKay's room. *He doesn't look scared. He kinda looks happy.*

Civil War projects packed three long tables along the back wall of the history room. The first display was a pen and ink sketch of Fort Sumter in Charleston, South Carolina with a typed report from *The Golden Book History of the United States*:

On April 12, 1861, a flash of light and a loud boom sounded at four-thirty in the morning. Confederate cannons opened fire. Union Sergeant James Chester later recalled, "Shot and shell went screaming

over Sumter as if an army of devils were swooping around it."

Surgeon Samuel Wylie Crawford later described the inside of the fort: "The flames of the burning quarters were still spreading, shooting upward amid the dense smoke as heavy masses of brick and masonry crumbled, and fell with loud noise. All of the woodwork had now been consumed. The heavy gates at the entrance, as well as the planking of the windows on the gorge, were gone, leaving access to the fort easy and almost unobstructed."

After hour upon hour of cannon blasts, Major Robert Anderson surrendered. One battle had ended, but a war had just begun.

The second exhibit showed watercolor paintings of four key figures of the American Civil War: President Abraham Lincoln, General Ulysses S. Grant, General Robert E. Lee, and Jefferson Davis. Another student had made a replica of a battlefield with a Barbie doll dressed as Clara Barton attending wounded Ken soldiers scattered across the field.

On the center table beside a popsicle-stick model of the Appomattox Court House sat Mark's Fort McKay. Sharp-pointed fencing and a locked gate barricaded log headquarters, bunk houses, and officer quarters. In the courtyard stood a flagpole with a miniature American flag. A stable with toy horses hugged the back corner, and a first-place blue ribbon dangled from the cherry-stained plywood.

Mr. McKay walked up behind us. "I could tell Mark put a lot of time and effort into his project."

So did Daddy, I thought, but for once kept my mouth shut.

The teacher put a hand on Mark's shoulder. "He's one of my most respectful students. I really enjoy having Mark in my class."

Daddy shook hands with Mr. McKay. "We're glad to hear that."

Mama grinned from ear to ear.

REFLECTIONS

A POINT TO PONDER

Did Mr. McKay change his opinion of Mark?

A PEARL FROM GOD

". . . *The LORD does not look at the things people look at. People look at the outward appearance, but the LORD looks at the heart.*" (1 Samuel 16:7)

A PRINCIPLE TO LIVE BY

In the Bible, the "heart" represents our mind, emotions, will, and conscience. Jesus told us in Mark 12:30-31 to love God with all our heart and to love other people as ourselves. Beloved, love God and people with all your heart — all your mind, emotions, will, and conscience.

Chapter 13:

Horseshoes

"Mark out a straight path for your feet so
that those who are weak and lame
will not fall but become strong."
(Hebrews 12:13 NLT)

Steve hobbled down the road on homemade crutches. His black dog, Rascal, trotted along beside him. Mark and I met him halfway between our houses.

I petted Rascal. "What happened?"

"Sprained my ankle playing football."

"Does it hurt?"

"Not much."

We moseyed back down the hill. The neighborhood looked like a postcard. Orange and yellow trees blazed under a cloudless sky. Goldenrods and black-eyed Susans edged the road. Through the woods, Granddaddy Eberhart's pond sparkled like diamonds in sunshine.

I took a deep breath. "I love Saturdays — especially in the fall."

Steve said, "Yeah, I like fall, too — fall and football. Alabama's playing Mississippi State this afternoon, you know."

I nodded like I knew. I didn't. "I hope we win."

Mark picked up four horseshoes. "Wanna play?"

"Sure," Steve said.

"I'll keep score," I offered.

A low hedge separated our yard from the Raymond's. Beside the hedge, Mark had hammered two steel stakes into the ground forty feet apart and marked out a pitching box and a pit around each stake. He kept the red horseshoes and handed Steve the blue ones.

Steve pulled a quarter from his pocket. "Heads or tails?"

"Tails," Mark called.

Steve flipped the coin.

"Heads," Mark said. "You first, Steve."

Steve pitched. CLANK! A dead ringer.

"Good throw!" I cheered from the hood of Daddy's jeep.

His second toss fell outside the pit.

Mark's turn. The first red shoe touched the stake; the second one hit the dirt with a thud.

"Let's see." I counted my fingers. "That's three points for Steve and one for Mark? Did I do that right?"

Steve shook his head. "Nope. Just three points for me. Maybe I better keep score, Jill. I went first last time, so you're first this round, Mark."

Mark tossed.

"Did Mark tell you we found a secret room at Karen Isbell's house?"

Steve nodded. "Yeah, wish I could see it."

"And I wrote a letter to James Ralph Johnson. That's the name we found on the wall. Daddy knew him in high school. He's a *really* famous author and artist now."

Steve's turn. "Did he write back?"

"Not yet. I just mailed it Tuesday."

Mark's turn. "Hey, Steve, I've been thinking about building a raft. You think your Granddaddy would let us put it on the pond?"

"That's a good idea. We could use it for swimming in the summertime and fishing all the time. Let's ask him when we're done."

"Okay. Thanks!"

Steve's turn.

"What's the score?" I asked.

"Fifteen to eleven," Steve said.

Mark's turn.

"Who's winning?"

"Steve is," Mark said.

Steve's turn.

"Ringer!" I hollered.

"You think Alabama will beat Mississippi State today?" Mark asked.

Steve tossed the second shoe. "Sure. Mississippi State's only won two games this whole season and lost four. It should be an easy win."

Mark's turn.

Steve's turn.

Mark's turn.

Steve's turn.

This game sure is takin' a long time, I thought. A yellow jacket landed on my knee. I screamed and jumped off the jeep.

Steve laughed. "What's the matter with you?"

"Bee. I don't like bees. Are your grandmama and Aunt Evelyn making popcorn balls and candied apples for Halloween on Monday?"

"Think so. They always do."

"Good! I love your grandmother's popcorn balls." Rip trotted over and rubbed his head against my jeans. I scratched his ears.

Mark's turn. Two good throws — a ringer and a leaner.

Steve's turn. "Ringer! That should win the game if you don't cancel me out."

Mark's turn. His first horseshoe leaned against the stake.

"Come on, Mark. You can do it!" I cheered.

The second one flew up, up, up into the air and down, down, down into the pit — less than an inch from the stake.

Steve threw both arms up, dropping crutches to the ground. "Game! Twenty-one to eighteen. Good game, Mark."

That night, I stared down the dark hallway, waiting for a signal from the bottom bunk. While studying for the ham radio test a couple of years back, Daddy had taught Mark and me Morse code and given us flashlights with code sending buttons. Sometimes we sent dit-dah messages before falling asleep.

I picked up my light and signaled:

–.–– ––– ..– (you)
.– .–– .– –.– . (awake)

–.–– . ... (yes)

– .... .. –. –.– (think)
.... . (he)
.–– .. .–.. .–.. (will)
.–– .–. .. – . (write)

.... ––– .–– . (hope)
... ––– (so)

––. ––– ––– –.. (good)
–. .. ––. .... – (night)
–– .– .–. –.– (Mark)

–. .. ––. .... – (night)
.––– .. .–.. .–.. (Jill)

96

REFLECTIONS

A POINT TO PONDER

What did Mark and I use to send messages?

_____ _____

A PEARL FROM GOD

"Long ago God spoke many times and in many ways to our ancestors through the prophets. And now in these final days, He has spoken to us through His Son . . ." (Hebrews 1:1-2 NLT)

A PRINCIPLE TO LIVE BY

In the Bible, God sent messages through angels, prophets, and His Son, Jesus. Today, God sends messages through His Word, the Holy Bible: *"For God so loved the world that He gave His one and only Son that whoever believes in Him shall not perish but have eternal life"* (John 3:16). Beloved, have you received and believed God's message?

Chapter 14:

Book and Letter

"And he had in his hand a little book..." (Revelation 10:2)

November came. Still no word from Mr. Johnson. Rocky told me to cheer up because he had good news: The National Football League had given a franchise to New Orleans to start a new team called the New Orleans Saints.

I rolled my eyes. "Well, whoop-de-doo."

On Saturday, Alabama rolled over LSU 21-0 and remained undefeated.

On Tuesday, the people of California elected a movie star named Ronald Reagan as their new governor. Walter Cronkite on the CBS evening news seemed to think that was a big deal. I wasn't sure why.

On Wednesday, I ran outside to meet Daddy's jeep as he pulled into the driveway. "Any mail for me today?" (Instead of a mailbox in the neighborhood, our mail came to a box at the post office. So, Daddy was our postman.)

"Not today, sugar."

On Saturday, we watched the moon pass between the earth and the sun — a total solar eclipse. That afternoon, Alabama eclipsed South Carolina, 24 to zip.

Days passed.

"Jill, it's the last out, so don't worry about a pop-fly. Just run when I hit the ball. Okay?"

I shot Mark a thumbs-up from first base.

The best baseball field in the neighborhood was Freddy and Steve's backyard. A pile of pine cones served as home plate. A rock was first, a hickory tree second, and a bare spot in the grass third.

It would be dark by five-thirty, and the sun had already dropped under Sand Mountain. We hurried to finish the game in the twilight.

Freddy pitched.

CRACK!

The ball flew over Freddy's head and dropped through the trees behind the second-base hickory. Steve scooped it off the ground and sprinted toward second. Inches before I tagged the bark, the ball tagged me.

"Out!" Steve yelled.

"Oh, man."

Headlights lit the field.

"Come on, Jill. There's Daddy."

Daddy stopped the jeep by the Eberhart's driveway. Mark grabbed his bat and glove. "See y'all tomorrow."

"Bye," Steve said.

I ran to the jeep. "I call front seat!"

Daddy moved a package from the passenger seat and tilted it forward for Mark to climb into the back. When I hopped in, he dropped the package addressed to Miss Jill Watson from Santa Fe, New Mexico in my lap. I ripped the brown paper and found an art gallery handout, a four-page, handwritten letter, and an autographed copy of *Anyone Can Live Off the Land*, written by James Ralph Johnson and illustrated by Edward Shenton.

REFLECTIONS

A POINT TO PONDER

On November 12, 1966, we watched the moon pass between the earth and the _____.

A PEARL FROM GOD

And God said, "Let there be lights in the vault of the sky to separate the day from the night . . . And it was so. God made two great lights — the greater light to govern the day and the lesser light to govern the night. He also made the stars. (Genesis 1:14-16)

A PRINCIPLE TO LIVE BY

John 1:1-4 tells us that *all* things were made by God. Beloved, thank God, the Creator, for the earth, sun, moon, and stars — and for Jesus, the Light of the world.

Chapter 15:

There is a Door

"*The secret things belong to the LORD our God, but the things revealed belong . . .*

to our children . . ."

(Deuteronomy 29:29)

Dear Jill,

I like your handwriting better than mine — so I hope you can read this. I've seen your father several times over the past years when we were in Fort Payne. Although he was a couple of years ahead of me in school, we did some Boy Scouting together and attended several small high school parties. I suspect my classmates remember me most clearly as having the most pimples per square inch of any kid in school. But, as they say, you can't judge a book by its cover. As a boy, I learned that I could do anything I really wanted to (as can anybody), and I've never changed my mind.

Fort Payne is one of those ideal places for a young person to live. People in towns that size know more about world affairs than citizens of New York City or other large cosmopolitan areas. There is little contamination of the air and land, and there is no end of challenging activities.

I'm sorry it took a while for me to answer. We returned last night from California and a week's delivering paintings to galleries. We do most such traveling in a Volkswagen Camper, so it's economical.

I couldn't stop smiling as I read your letter. Congratulations on finding the hidden room! Instead of giving you the answers to your good questions, it's my pleasure (and more fun for you, I believe) to simply offer clues to help you unfold the "secrets" of Willow Springs.

However, I must tell you the first secret outright lest you break your necks. THERE IS A DOOR, dear children. I can't believe you climbed through that tiny window! Please DO NOT use the window entrance again, even with your parents' permission. Search this letter carefully to find a clue that will lead you to a hidden door.

I hope you and your family enjoy _Anyone Can Live Off the Land_, published in 1961. I expect to write little in the future since painting has been my interest since childhood. I love it and work until 2 or 3 A.M. seven days a week because of my enthusiasm. (Yes, I painted the mural of Willow Springs my senior year of high school.)

I studied art for four years under Alida Townes, a product of the Chicago Art Institute, as well as shorter courses with various artists. Because the principle behind my art is: "If you cannot live with a painting and enjoy it daily, then there's no point in having it around," I love to paint the clean, sunny scenes of the Southwest.

You may also find it interesting that three of my wife's books were filmed by Walt Disney Studios. As a matter of fact, _Run, Light Buck, Run_ aired on NBC's Walt Disney's

Wonderful World of Color on March 13th earlier this year. Did you happen to see it?

I hope this letter "swings the door wide open" for you. Let me know when you find it, and I'll send the next clue. Give my regards to Winfred and your mother.

Cordially

James Ralph Johnson

REFLECTIONS

A POINT TO PONDER

In his letter, Mr. Johnson told us that the hidden room had a _____.

A PEARL FROM GOD

"Here I am! I stand at the door and knock. If anyone hears My voice and opens the door, I will come in and eat with that person, and they with Me." (Revelation 3:20)

A PRINCIPLE TO LIVE BY

In Revelation 3:20, Jesus invites His followers into deeper friendship with Him. Beloved, did you know that Jesus wants to be your BFF: best friend forever? Knock, knock, knock. Will you open your heart's door and fellowship with Him every day?

Chapter 16:

Think

"Finally, brothers and sisters, whatever is true . . .
whatever is right . . . think about such things."
(Philippians 4:8)

"Read it again," Karen said.

I slumped against her bookcase in the upstairs hallway. "I've read it three times already."

"I know, but we still haven't found the clue."

"Alright." I turned back to page one: "I like your handwriting better than mine — so I hope you can read this. I've seen your father several times over the years."

"Here, let me see that." Mark snatched the letter from my hands. "I've heard this thing so many times I know it by heart. Just think a minute. What do we know so far?"

"We know there's a door . . . somewhere," I said.

Karen pointed toward the bathroom. "And it has to be between the bathroom and that window, but the whole wall is nothing but bookshelves."

Mark jumped up. "Wait a minute. Maybe the door's not in the wall. Maybe it's a trap door in the floor or the ceiling! What room's under the secret room?"

"The living room," Karen said. "Come on. Let's go!"

We flew down the stairs to the living room and stared at the chandelier hanging from the high ceiling.

I squinted. "See any cracks up there that look like a trap door?"

Karen shook her head. "Nope. Besides, the ceiling is too high. We'd have to use a ladder, and Mr. Johnson sounded like the door wasn't dangerous — like you could just walk right into the room."

Mark looked at Karen. "Or drop into it."

She yelled, "Mama, can we go up in the attic?"

A chuckled floated from the kitchen. "Sure, honey, but you'll need a flashlight."

I looked around the spooky attic. "So, where would the secret room be?"

Karen shined the beam this way and that. "Uh, that way's the front of the house, and the room is in the center. So, let's look over there."

I nodded toward a dot of light. "There's the tiny half window over the front porch. The secret room should start about ten feet back from it."

Mark looked surprised. "Good thinking, Jill."

I liked his praise.

Mark shoved an old trunk with a broken hinge out of the way. "Look under here."

The light sent a roach scurrying. Karen and I squealed.

She traced the boards with the beam. "Nope. Nothing here."

We searched right.

Left.

In front.

Behind.

And started over again.

And again.

And again.

Karen sighed. "The room's tiny. If it's not here, there must not be a trap door after all."

"Maybe your mama could help," I suggested.

We scrambled down the narrow attic steps and hurried downstairs to the kitchen. Mrs. Isbell stood at the double sink washing dishes.

Wow! I thought. *Our whole house would fit in here.*

A wide, stone fireplace surrounded by tall cabinets filled one wall. The stove, double ovens, and more cabinets lined an adjacent wall, and a large, round, oak table and heavy, wooden chairs sat in the center of the room. On the far wall, a door led to the hallway. On the near side, a door opened into the butler's pantry and dining room. A back door led to a small, cheery sun porch with church pews from the old First Baptist Church sanctuary.

Mrs. Isbell caught me looking at the porch. "Whenever I get a minute to sit down, that's my favorite place to read the paper or just sit and watch the children play. Did you find anything in the attic?"

"No, ma'am," Karen answered.

"Ask her," I whispered.

"Mama, will you read this letter, please, and help us find the clue for the door?"

"Well, I think Mr. Johnson wants you children to find it, but I might offer a clue to the clue."

"Huh?"

She smiled. "Name all the things you found in the room."

"The painting," Karen said.

"A Boy Scout Handbook," Mark said.

"Bookshelves and tons of books," I added, "and an old Bible."

Karen picked up an apple. "And a desk and chairs. Y'all want an apple?"

I shook my head.

"So, why don't you reread the letter and search for those things you just named."

"Yes, ma'am!"

REFLECTIONS

A POINT TO PONDER

Mrs. Isbell offered a _____ to the clue in the Willow Springs mystery.

A PEARL FROM GOD

"My goal is that they may be encouraged in heart and united in love, so that they may have the full riches of complete understanding, in order that they may know the mystery of God, namely Christ, in whom are hidden all the treasures of wisdom and knowledge." (Colossians 2:2-3)

A PRINCIPLE TO LIVE BY

The Bible tells us that God kept a mystery hidden for ages. The mystery? His plan of salvation through Jesus, conceived "before the foundation of the world" (Ephesians 1:4). God's plan has now been revealed and fulfilled. What Good News! Beloved, boldly tell others God's mysterious Good News: God's Son, Jesus, was born. He lived on earth. He died in the place of you and me and absorbed our sin. He arose from death. He's alive! He went back to heaven. He will return to earth one day. Therefore, believe, receive eternal life, and be saved from God's judgment of sin!

Chapter 17:

Undercover

"On that day the Book . . . was read aloud . . . and there it was found written . . ." (Nehemiah 13:1)

Karen wedged between Mark and me on the front steps and took a bite of the crisp apple. "I'll read it this time," she said.

Dear Jill,

I like your handwriting better than mine — so I hope you can read this. I've seen your father several times over the past years when we were in Fort Payne. Although he was a couple of years ahead of me in school, we did some Boy Scouting together . . ."

"Hold on," Mark said. "Boy Scouting. We found that handbook. Keep going."

". . . and attended several small high school parties. I suspect my classmates remember me most clearly as having the most pimples per square inch of any kid in school. But, as they say, you can't judge a book by its cover."

"Book!" I shouted. "Mr. Johnson said *you can't judge a book by its cover*. You think that's the clue? There's tons of books in the room."

Karen shook her head. "The clue to find the door to get *in* the room wouldn't be inside the room we're trying to get into."

"Oh, yeah." I pounded my forehead with my fist.

"What's the next line?" Mark asked.

"As a boy, I learned that I could do anything I really wanted to, as can anyone."

"Well, I really wanna find the door into the secret room," he said. "Let's go back upstairs."

We sat on the floor, staring at the bookcase.

I leaned against the wall. "Just think. The secret room is right on the other side of those books. We're so close, but how in the world do we get in?"

Karen shook her head.

I pulled *The Story of Mankind* by Hendrik Van Loon from the bottom shelf. A round sticker on the front cover read: First John Newbery Medal winner, 1922. "There sure are lots of books here. Are all of 'em yours?"

Mark's forehead crinkled. "Hey, were any of these books already here when you moved in?"

"Uh . . . I don't know." Karen leaned over the banister. "Hey, Mama! Were any books already here when we moved in?"

"What, honey?"

"I said, 'Were any of these books already in the bookcase when we moved in?'"

"Top shelf."

"Ma'am?"

"The Bethunes left all the books on the top shelf for you and Laura and Chuck."

"The top shelf?" Mark jumped to his feet. "I've got an idea!"

"What?" I asked.

"*Don't judge a book by its cover*. Maybe it's not a book *in* the room. Maybe our answer's in a book *outside* the room. Help me look."

Karen picked up *Little House in the Big Woods* by Laura Ingalls Wilder. "What are we looking for?"

I snatched The *Milly-Molly-Mandy Storybook* by Joyce Lankester Brisley. "I don't know. Maybe a handwritten note or an underlined sentence or a picture or a map or something?"

"Look at this." Karen showed me a sketch of a hollow tree trunk topped with a board roof. A little door with leather hinges cut into one side.

"What's that?"

"It's where Pa made a smoker for the salted deer meat, and Laura fed the fire with green hickory chips to make it smoke like crazy."

"What does that have to do with anything?"

Karen shrugged. "It just kinda looked like a secret door to me."

"Not those books," Mark said. "The top shelf. Your mama said the Bethunes left all the books on the *top* shelf."

I stood on my tiptoes and touched *Just William* by Richmal Crompton. Karen grabbed a stool from Laura's room and picked up *Bright Island* by Mabel L. Robinson.

"You know, in old movies, sometimes they used fake books to hide money or valuable jewels or to open the door into a secret passageway. Wouldn't it be funny if . . ."

POP!

SCREACH!

SCRAPE!

When Mark tilted *The Incredible Adventures of Professor Branestawm* by Norman Hunter, the entire bookcase swung open — the door to the secret room.

I jumped back.

Karen squealed and fell off the stool.

Mrs. Isbell called, "Y'all okay up there?"

"Yes ma'am," Karen hollered. She put her finger to her lips. We crept through the open bookcase and quietly closed it behind us.

"We found it!" I whispered.

She grabbed my hands, and we skipped ring-around-the-rosie circles.

I put a hand over my heart. "Well, I do declare, Mrs. Snodgrass. I've neva seen such a sight in all my born days! A swingin' bookcase and a hidden room."

Karen fanned her face with an imaginary fan. "Why, yes, Miss Maude. It's been our family secret for generations!"

We giggled. Mark wore a big grin. "You gotta write Mr. Johnson and tell him we found the door."

Dear Mr. Johnson,

Thank you for writing back and thank you for the book. Karen, Mark, and I worked together and found the clue in your letter: "Don't judge a book by its cover." It took us a while, but we finally figured out that the bookcase is the door. Who came up with that idea?

We're ready for the next clue. Please write back fast.

Sincerely,
Jill

P.S. Mrs. Weatherly at the library helped us gather these old pictures and articles about DeKalb County. We hope you like them. It was Mama's idea.

REFLECTIONS

A POINT TO PONDER

The secret door was disguised as a

_____.

A PEARL FROM GOD

"You, LORD, are our Father. We are the clay, You are the potter; we are all the work of Your hand." (Isaiah 64:8)

A PRINCIPLE TO LIVE BY

Beloved, God made you according to His wonderful design to serve His good purposes. Like clay in the hands of a potter, yield to God. Let Him shape you into all that He designed you to be and do.

Chapter 18:

In the Meantime

"Wait for the LORD; be strong and take heart and wait for the LORD." (Psalm 27:14)

Mama cut her eyes toward me. "I know it's hard to wait, sugar, but Mr. Johnson's a busy man. He said he'd write back. I'm sure he will when he can. So, in the meantime, why don't you think about something other than that room at Karen's house — like your piano, for instance."

I made a sour-pickle face.

The Thanksgiving holidays and another week had passed since we mailed the second letter to Mr. Johnson. Bright leaves had fallen into brown piles under bare-limbed trees. Last Saturday, the University of Southern Mississippi had fallen to the Crimson Tide (still undefeated). Tomorrow, Bama would face Auburn, their biggest rival.

Mama and I headed down Alabama Avenue toward my Friday afternoon piano lesson at Mrs. Roberta White's house. Earlier that fall, Mama told my piano teacher that getting me to practice was as hard as pulling teeth. So, Mrs. White had replaced Beethoven and Bach with modern tunes like "Moon River" by Henry Mancini and "Love is Blue" by Andre' Popp.

I pulled a folded paper from my book satchel. "We got a Scholastic Books order sheet today."

"Did you find anything you like?"

"Yes, ma'am. Two. *Mystery of the Haunted Pool* by Phyllis Whitney and *The Velvet Room* by Zilpha Keatley Snyder. Can I order both?"

"*May* I order both. How much are they?"

"*Mystery of the Haunted Pool* is 45¢ and *The Velvet Room is* 55¢."

"Probably so but ask your daddy tonight."

At the brick house on the corner of Alabama and 8th Street, I hopped from the car and slipped through the new sliding-glass door plastered with paper-lace doilies. (One of the Walker boys, running full speed ahead, had busted through the old one. Doilies now served as warning signs: "There is a door here, children!") I tip-toed to the couch and waited for Laurie Sauls to finish her lesson.

"Very nice, Laurie," Mrs. White was saying. "Keep up the good work. I'll see you next week."

Laurie smiled. "Hey, Jill."

I waved.

Mrs. White patted the bench after she left. "Okay, Miss Jill, your turn. Let's see how "Moon River" is coming along."

I played the no-flats-no-sharps key of C measures with a few blunders but fumbled my way through the A flat major parts with four tricky flats.

The always-kind Mrs. White encouraged, "I can tell you've been practicing. Let's keep working on this piece a while longer."

On the way home, Mama asked, "How was your lesson today?"

"Good. Mrs. White said she could tell I'd practiced. What's Mark doing?"

"When I left, he and Steve were in the woods behind the house working on some sort of project."

I found Mark and Steve waist deep in a rectangular hole.

"Whatcha doing?"

Mark thrust a shovel into the dirt. "Makin' an underground hideout."

"Like a fallout shelter? It looks like you're diggin' a grave."

"It's gonna have a fireplace and everything," Steve said and tossed a shovel full of red clay. Rascal dodged the flying dirt and laid back down.

"Does Daddy know y'all are digging a hole? You know this isn't our land. It's Mr. Raymond's."

Mark kept working. "I know, but Mr. Raymond won't care. Besides, he never comes down here."

"Can I help?"

Mark wiped sweat from his face, leaving a muddy streak. "Only two shovels."

"I could run get a rake and pull the dirt away from the edge."

"Okay."

They shoveled and I raked until dusk fell over the mountain.

"Did Mark tell you we found the door into the secret room?"

"Yep. I wonder what the next clue will be?"

"I think it might have something to do with that Boy Scout Handbook," Mark said.

Steve emptied the shovel. "If it does, I can help. I know all about the Boy Scouts in DeKalb County."

I tossed a rock to the side. "You do? How?"

"Grandmama's friend, Mrs. Van Allen, told me."

"What'd she say?"

"She said Mr. Beck started the first DeKalb County Boy Scout troop down in Collinsville in 1930, and a couple of years later, he started a second troop in Fort Payne. Mr. Raymond and Mr. Owen . . . and let me think . . . Mr. Shugart, Mr. Crow, and Mr. Mann . . . anyway, several of the men in Fort Payne were the boys in that troop."

I rubbed my cold nose on my sleeve. "Did she say anything about James Ralph Johnson?"

"Nope, not that I remember. But she said that Colonial Milford Howard — you know the one that built Howard's Chapel at the Park?"

Mark and I nodded.

"He deeded 'em a whole bunch of land by Little River. Mr. Beck and Troop No. 24 built a cabin up there. Colonial Howard gave 'em the timber and rocks to do it."

Mark leaned on his shovel. "I'd like to do that — build a cabin."

"She said the Depression took a toll on the Boy Scouts just like everybody else, and they couldn't afford the taxes. So, they lost the land in 1936. But guess what? This year, exactly thirty years later, the Choccolocco Boy Scout Council bought it back."

The CLANG! CLANG! CLANG! of Mama's brass bell broke through the chilly air.

Mark crawled out of the hole. "Time to go."

"I hope supper's ready," I said. "I'm starvin'."

REFLECTIONS

A POINT TO PONDER

Even though the Boy Scouts lost their
_____, in time, they got it back.

A PEARL FROM GOD

*"This is what the Sovereign LORD says: My people
. . . I will bring you back to the land of Israel . . . I will settle
you in your own land." (Ezekiel 37:12,14)*

A PRINCIPLE TO LIVE BY

God's people, the Jews, had been scattered
away from their homeland for over 2,400 years when
Israel became a nation again on May 14, 1948. Beloved,
God is the Restorer. All His promises come true. Study
the Bible. Know God promises and put high hopes in the
Promise Keeper.

Chapter 19:

Like Heaven

"What no eye has seen, what no ear has heard, and what no mind can conceive — the things that God has prepared for those who love Him."
(1 Corinthians 2:9)

The Iron Bowl at Legion Field was no contest. Alabama, led by Coach Bear Bryant and quarterback Kenny "Snake" Stabler, clobbered the Auburn tigers 31 to 0, leaving no hopes for a bowl game for the Plainsmen and Coach "Shug" Jordan. Bama, on the other hand, set their eyes on the Sugar Bowl.

That afternoon, Mark left me cleaning my room (a weekly chore that I had put off till the last minute) and walked across the highway to Chip Blanton's house.

I gathered a mountain of dirty clothes from the floor and stuffed them in the hamper in the hall, made my bed, dusted the chest of drawers and dresser, and watered the philodendron under my lamp.

"Mama!" I hollered. "I'm done. Will you come check my room so I can go play?"

"Please?" she called back.

"Please," I said and kicked a dirty sock under the bed.

The trail to Granddaddy Eberhart's pond bypassed the Raymonds' grumpy dogs and took me near the end of our road. Looking both ways, I crossed the highway and started into the new neighborhood. I'd never ventured there alone because, even though our neighbors' dogs were grumpy, Chip's neighbors' dogs were downright vicious. Mark always let me hide behind him.

Made it, I thought when I stepped into Chip's yard. But I thought wrong. Two barking, growling, snapping dogs were suddenly behind me. My heart pounded like a kettle drum.

Just ignore 'em and keep walking. They'll go away, I told myself. Wrong again. The black one snapped at my leg and sank his sharp teeth into the side of my knee. I flew to the door shaking like a dry leaf and banged hard for somebody to let me in.

When Chip opened the door, he said, "What's wrong with you? You're as white as a ghost?"

I ran straight to Mark, trying not to cry.

"What's the matter?" he asked.

"That dogs bit me."

"Are you hurt?"

"My knee hurts, but I don't see any blood."

That night, Mama called the owners to make sure the dog had been vaccinated for rabies. Mark said that he would make sure I never crossed the highway alone again. Rocky helped me set the supper table without being asked, and Daddy decided it would be a good night to decorate the Fraser fir Christmas tree soaking in a bucket of water on the back porch.

Everybody sure is being nice, I thought.

After supper, Mama stood atop the red stepstool and handed down boxes of lights and ornaments from the cabinet over the bathtub. Rocky, Mark, and I carried them to the living room where Daddy had a fire snap-crackle-and-popping in the fireplace.

The tree-decorating routine was the same every year. I used Mama's little gooseneck, brass watering can to fill the tree stand while Daddy tested lights. My favorites were the bubble lights and frosted snowballs. Last year, Mama had added a string of colorful lanterns.

Rocky helped Daddy string the lights and glittery, gold garland around the tree. Mama made sure both were spaced and draped perfectly. I threw one of the long gold ropes around my neck and pretended it was a fancy boa.

When the lights and garland met her approval, Mama unwrapped ornaments. I hung a small plastic manger scene from Sunday School on a low limb. Mark picked a silver half-ball filled with a jolly, red Santa. Rocky chose the large, gold ball from Helen, Georgia that had been hand-painted with a snow-covered cabin with smoke curling from the chimney.

Store-bought and handmade ornaments of every shape and color filled the tree.

Filigree balls.

Glossy teardrops.

Santa's elves from Aunt Dot.

Jingle bells.

Foil stars.

Shiny globes.

Snowmen.

Jolly old Saint Nick.

A blue-feathered peacock.

Gingerbread men.

Candy canes.

Crystal snowflakes.

Angels.

Rudolf with his glowing red nose.

And a drummer boy, pa rum pa pum pum.

Long, silver icicles added the finishing touch. Rocky threw a handful onto the tree and joked, "I think they look better this way."

"One at time," Mama said and meticulously draped a single, silver thread over a branch.

When icicles hung from tiptop to floor, Daddy set the silver, glass topper in the place of honor, and Mama spread the white, glittered blanket around the bottom.

Picture perfect.

The living room glowed in Christmas-tree and fire light. Mark and I sprawled on the floor with our heads stuck under the tree, looking up through the branches. It smelled like a pine forest.

Rocky walked by. "What are y'all doing?"

"Looking at the lights," Mark said.

I scooted closer to Mark. "Come see, Rocky."

He dropped down beside us, and we stared at the green, red, blue, and gold twinkles. The fire hissed in the fireplace.

I twirled a foil star. "Is this what heaven's like?"

"Whatcha mean?" Rocky asked.

"Safe and happy and beautiful with the people you love?"

He looked at me and then back at the tree. "Yeah, I think so."

REFLECTIONS

A POINT TO PONDER

I asked Rocky if _____ is safe, happy, and beautiful.

A PEARL FROM GOD

". . . the city of pure gold . . . with every kind of precious stone . . . The twelve gates were twelve pearls . . . The great street of the city was of gold . . . No longer will there be any curse . . . The throne of God and of the Lamb will be in the city, and His servants will serve Him. And they will see His face . . ."
(Revelation 21:18-22:4)

A PRINCIPLE TO LIVE BY

God promised a beautiful and beyond-wonderful heaven, and He provided the way to get there: trust in Jesus — the only Way to everlasting life.

Chapter 20:

The Riddle

"Let me tell you a riddle . . ." (Judges 14:12)

Two weeks before Christmas, my friend, Mary, and I met at Fort Payne Drugstore on the corner of Gault Avenue and 1st Street. Her uncle, Mr. Carden, was one of the pharmacists and owners. Since second grade, we had Christmas shopped together. The ladies at the drugstore always wrapped our packages (no matter what store they came from).

Our town's traditional Santa (who remarkably resembled Mr. John Blake from Adamsburg) strolled up and down Gault Avenue, visiting stores and asking children if they had been naughty or nice. When I was three, he told me that I sure was a pretty, little girl. I embarrassed Mama when I answered, "I know it."

As fifth graders, we felt way too old to talk to Santa Claus. So, every time bells jingled, Mary and

I ducked into the nearest store and hid until the red suit passed on by.

At the supper table that night, Mark said, "Santa Claus stopped by Eberhart's Grocery this afternoon on his way back to the North Pole."

I took a big bite of a toasted cheese sandwich with crispy bacon. "He did?"

"Yeah, and Frank and I sat on his knee and told him what we wanted for Christmas."

Hmm, I thought, *they're eighth graders. Maybe I'm not too old for Santa after all.*

Sunday evening, a week before Christmas Day, Mama and Daddy let Mark and me set up trays for supper in the playroom. We watched the premiere of the CBS television special: "How the Grinch Stole Christmas," based on Dr. Seuss's 1957 children's book. The voices of both the Grinch and the narrator were performed by the English actor Boris Karloff. When Thurl Ravenscroft sang "You're a Mean One, Mr. Grinch," I cracked up and said, "That's the deepest voice I've ever heard!"

The next day, Daddy held my hand as we walked the short distance from his office over Owen's Fort Payne Hardware Store to the Post Office on Gault Avenue South. He caught his black fedora when a blast of cold wind nearly sailed it down the sidewalk like Santa's sleigh over the night sky.

We hurried up the concrete steps. Fort Payne's red-brick Post Office was built in 1936. A white cupola and weathervane topped the shiny, metal roof. Inside, a 1938 mural by Harwood Steiger entitled "Harvest of Fort Payne," decorated one wall. The painting portrayed the rural south. A farmhouse sat near a cottonfield where three bent figures picked snow-white cotton. Chickens pecked the red-dirt road, and across the way, horses pulled a sorghum-cane press while men stirred the boiling, sweet juice over a hot fire. Lookout Mountain stood guard in the background. I loved that painting. It reminded me of my granddaddy's farm.

Daddy pulled a packed keyring from his pants' pocket and opened Box 282. Thumbing through the mail, a hand-addressed envelope postmarked December 10th, New Mexico brought a smile to his face. He handed the letter to me.

Dear Jill, Mark, and Karen,

Wow! Guess who is at the top of my list of wonderful people. The DeKalb County information and photographs that you sent delight me to no end. Please tell Mrs. Weatherly thank you for gathering the articles. I have seen only a few of the photos before, and since I have always wondered about the history of various places in the county, this will give me a chance to find the answers. Thanks for underlining my father's name. I'll have many pleasant hours studying the things you sent.

The first chance we get, we'll stop by for a short visit. Your house must have about the nicest view in the county, and I would thoroughly enjoy seeing it and your family.

Well, enough of my rambling. I'm sure you three are chomping at the bit for the next clue. Here you go, kids:

Karen and Mark's little sister, Jill,
From the spring, looked up the hill.
Spotted a window on second floor,
Moved a book and found the door.
Now this is what you need to do,
Add you + books + scouts for clue.

Let me know when you've solved the riddle, and I'll send you the last clue to the secrets of Willow Springs. Happy sleuthing!

Cordially

James Ralph Johnson

REFLECTIONS

A POINT TO PONDER

Mr. Johnson sent a _____ as the next clue.

A PEARL FROM GOD

The proverbs of Solomon son of David, king of Israel: for the gaining of wisdom and instruction . . . knowledge and discretion to the young . . . for understanding proverbs and parables, the sayings and riddles of the wise." (Proverbs 1:1-6)

A PRINCIPLE TO LIVE BY

In modern day translations of the Bible, Proverbs is divided into thirty-one chapters — a chapter of God's unmatched wisdom for each day of the month. Proverbs 9:10 tells us that wisdom begins with fear or great respect for the LORD. Beloved, I challenge you to grow in God's wisdom by reading one chapter of Proverbs each day for the next thirty-one days. Ready, set, go!

Chapter 21:

White Christmas

"And He says to the snow, 'Fall on the earth'. . ."
(Job 37:6)

Christmas Day.

It was still dark outside when I jumped from bed, stepped into my slippers, and rushed to the living room. Mark was adding a log to the crackling fire.

"How long have you been up?"

"About thirty minutes. Look what I got." He held out a Swiss Army knife. "See what's in your stocking."

Among Mama and Daddy's Christmas-Day rules were:

> #1. We couldn't wake them up before six o'clock.
>
> #2. We couldn't open any presents before they said so.
>
> #3. We could look in our stockings anytime we wanted to.

I dug past the tangerine and peppermint candy and pulled something round from the toe of the stocking. It was a gold-rimmed compact. The hand-painted scene on the front and back depicted a classical ballet class. A white-haired gentleman leaning on a walking cane held the attention of a roomful of young ladies in colorful tutus and pointe shoes.

I gasped. "Oh, look, Mark!"

"What is it?"

I popped the lid open. "It's a mirror."

"That's nice."

When Daddy's slippers patted down the hall, I hollered, "Merry Christmas!"

"Merry Christmas, lil'un," he answered on his way to the kitchen to start the percolator. "Thanks for starting the fire, Mark."

"You're welcome."

"Is Mama up yet?" I asked.

"She's combing her hair."

"Can we wake Rocky up?"

"Wait till your mama gets in here. Have y'all looked outside?"

I beat Mark to the window. "Snow!"

Most years in the South, we only dream of a white Christmas, but this year our dreams had come true. Through the night, snowflakes had swirled over Lookout Mountain, laying a white blanket on the ground and trees.

Daddy sat in the rocker by the fire, sipping hot A&P coffee from a black rooster mug.

A few years back, after saving money for a new set of everyday dishes, our folks brought home samples of two different patterns of Pennsylvania Pottery from Kelly's Gift Shop. Mama liked the heart-and-flower design. Daddy preferred the black rooster. Mama said that she didn't like anything with chickens because they pecked her toes when she was a little girl. In the end, she got her full set of heart-and-flower dinner platters, cups, saucers, dessert plates, and serving pieces; Daddy got one black rooster coffee cup.

While Mama grabbed a pen and pad of paper from the kitchen, Mark and I ran to wake Rocky. "Get up, Rocky! It's Christmas!"

"Christmas gift!" he hollered from the top bunk.

"That doesn't count!" Mark argued. "It's Christmas *Eve* gift, and that was yesterday." (The "Christmas Eve Gift" tradition was: The first one to say Christmas Eve gift on Christmas Eve Day got an early present.)

I snuggled next to Mama on the love seat. Her long hair was neatly combed into a bun at the top of her head. She wrapped an arm around me and said, "Merry Christmas, sugar. Ok, y'all can open gifts now, but don't forget to tell me what's in each box and who gave it to you so you can write thank-you notes this afternoon."

Rule #4: Write thank-you notes Christmas afternoon for the gifts you received Christmas morning.

I ran to the tree and a grabbed the present that I'd made in Mrs. Robinson's classroom. "Here, Mama, open mine first."

She untied the green ribbon and pulled a Mason jar from glittered tissue paper. "What's this?"

"Instant Russian tea. I made it. See? The recipe's taped to the jar: Two cups of tang, one pack of lemonade mix, a half cup of instant tea, one teaspoon cinnamon, one and half teaspoons of powdered cloves, and a cup of sugar. Just mix together and add two heaping teaspoons to a cup of hot water. It tastes really good!"

She kissed my cheek. "Thank you, Jill. I'll try a cup at breakfast."

Before I unwrapped a silver-foiled box with a red, velvet bow, I opened an envelope marked "Miss Tamara Jill Watson." The card inside had yellow roses on the front:

Dearest Jill,

The pitcher and three small glasses were given to your daddy's father when we first married. Your great-grandmother Watson (Minnie Cox Watson, born in 1869) gave them to him. She had sold something when she was a young girl to get them. As you'll notice by looking at the bottom of the pitcher, it's blown glass. Put them in your hope chest, then maybe you can give them to one of your grandchildren.

I love you,
Grandmother

REFLECTIONS

A POINT TO PONDER

What was our fourth Christmas rule? Always write _____ notes.

A PEARL FROM GOD

"Give thanks in all circumstances; for this is God's will for you in Christ Jesus." (1 Thessalonians 5:18)

A PRINCIPLE TO LIVE BY

An attitude of gratitude pleases God. Today, beloved, thank God for His love, blessings, and watch care over you, and be quick to thank others as well for the things they do for you.

Chapter 22:

Common Denominator

"Rich and poor have this in common: The LORD is the Maker of them all." (Proverbs 22:2)

Mark's chin rested in his hand (something he did when he was thinking). "Add you plus books plus scouts for clue. What do you think that means?"

I shrugged. "Ask Freddy. He's smart."

"Good idea."

Three days after Christmas was sunny and forty-five degrees, but patches of snow still clung to the shadows. Bundled in warm jackets, knit caps, and gloves, we hurried up the road to the Eberhart's house and found Steve splitting wood and Freddy stacking it.

Freddy waved. "Hey. What are y'all doing?"

I waved back. "We need your help solving a riddle."

Steve swung the ax over his head. A powerful blow buried the ax head into a log. "Did you get another letter from Mr. Johnson?"

"Yeah, and his clue this time is a riddle. Wanna hear?"

"Sure."

"Now this is what you need to do: Add you plus books plus scouts for clue."

Steve wiggled the ax loose. "You and the books and the Scout Handbook were all in that secret room. Maybe the next clue's hidden in there somewhere."

"Maybe," Mark said and stood another log on end.

Freddy shook his head. "But he said to *add* those things together to get the clue. I think it's like a math problem: A plus B plus C equals something, and that *something* is your clue."

"You're smart, Freddy," I said.

He grinned.

I tossed a wedge of wood on the stack. "Y'all wanna go down to the pond and see if it's still frozen?"

Steve wiped sweat from his forehead. "We gotta finish this wood first."

Mark reached for the ax. "We'll help."

Rascal ran ahead of us as we walked to Granddaddy Eberhart's fishing pond. He chased a rabbit across the pasture and into the woods.

At the pond, Steve broke a thin sheet of ice with his boot. "Remember when the whole pond froze over last winter?"

Mark nodded. "Yeah, we were walking on it and it started cracking."

Freddy laughed. "Sounded like jet planes flying over."

"It scared me to death," I said. "I thought we were all gonna drown."

The boys laughed.

Rascal trotted back to Steve. He patted his head. "The Birmingham News said that day last January was the coldest day in Alabama history. Twenty-seven degrees below zero in New Market."

Mark tossed a rock in the pond. "Daddy said it was eleven below in Valley Head that day."

"Mark, tell 'em what happened to Mr. Johnson during the war."

"Did y'all know Mr. Johnson sent Jill a book?"

"Yeah, she showed us," Freddy said.

"Well, the first chapter is 'How to Stay Warm in the Wilderness,' and he told a story about participating in training maneuvers with the Royal Air Force officers in England when he was in the United States Marine Corps. Mr. Johnson had to play the part of an enemy parachutist trying to escape through the fields, and his job was to sneak across twenty-five miles undetected to a secret rendezvous."

Freddy's eyes widened. "That would be hard."

"Yeah, and he said it was really cold, and he was exhausted after climbing through wet brush and fields the first night. So, on the second night, he was too slow and got caught. They threw him in the mock jail until the maneuvers were over. He went on to say that three of the most important things you need to have when you're living off the land are charred cotton, a pocketknife, and a piece of flint."

We walked on around the pond. "Charred cotton?" Steve asked.

"Yeah, to build a fire. You hold the knife about an inch above the charred cotton and strike it with the flint. The sparks will catch the cotton on fire. And you know the rest. We've done it a hundred times — blow gently and add shredded bark to the flame, and as the fire grows, add small sticks, then bigger ones until the fire's as big as you need."

Steve picked up a stick. Rascal grabbed the other end with his mouth. "Yeah, we've built lots of fires, but we've never used cotton before. Let's try it next time."

"Mr. Johnson was a major in the Marines." Mark said. "He served in Hawaii and in the battle of Iwo Jima and in the Japanese occupation forces in World War II."

I kicked a dirt clod. "Daddy was in the occupations forces, too. He sent Mama a fancy jewelry box from Okinawa and a silk kimono that he had made special just for her. And guess what? He paid for the kimono with a carton of cigarettes."

After supper, Mark and I played chess on the floor in front of the fireplace. I made a face when he captured my knight with a bishop.

"You know, I've been thinking," I said. "Freddy said to look at the riddle like a math problem, and Rocky's like some kind of math genius. He scored almost perfect on the math part of the ACT. We oughta ask him."

"Okay."

We found Rocky at his desk reading the latest edition of "Sports Illustrated." A picture of the seven-foot-two-inch-tall UCLA college-basketball star Lew Alcindor was on the cover.

I tapped his shoulder. "Rocky, will you help us with a math problem?"

"Sure. Whatcha got?"

I handed him Mr. Johnson's letter and pointed to the riddle. "Freddy said to think of it like a math problem — that A plus B plus C equals the clue."

Rocky studied the riddle. "Children," he said and handed the letter back.

"Huh?"

"It's not an equation; it's the common denominator between you and the books and scouting. A common denominator is a feature shared by all members of a group. You're *children*. The books are *children's* classics. Scouting is for *children*. Your next clue is *children*."

I punched Mark's arm. "See! Told ya he's a genius!"

REFLECTIONS

A POINT TO PONDER

Rocky quickly figured out that Mr. Johnson's next clue was _____.

A PEARL FROM GOD

"Jesus said, 'Let the little children come to Me, and do not hinder them, for the kingdom of heaven belongs to such as these." (Matthew 19:14)

A PRINCIPLE TO LIVE BY

The Bible emphasizes how important family and children are to God. The Apostle Paul wrote in 1 Timothy 4:12: *"Don't let anyone look down on you because you are young, but be an example for believers in speech, in conduct, in love, in faith, and in purity."* You may be young, beloved, but God is able to use you as a good example to your family and friends.

Chapter 23:

The Accident

"It was simply an accident permitted by God. . ."

(Exodus 21:13 NLT)

"Oh no!" Mama cried. "I'm so sorry to hear that."

(Pause)

"Yes, we'll certainly be praying for Karen. Thanks for calling, Arlene."

(Pause)

"Okay. Keep us posted, please. Bye now."

Mark and I had been sitting at the kitchen table drinking Pet milk and eating graham crackers smeared with Peter Pan peanut butter when the phone rang. A month had passed since Christmas.

On January 2nd, Alabama had pummeled Nebraska 34 to 7 in the Sugar Bowl played at Tulane Stadium in New Orleans. Although undefeated and the SEC champions, the Crimson Tide was not named national champions. Voters awarded the title to Notre

Dame, coached by Ara Parseghian. Bumper stickers around our state read: "In your heart you know we're No. 1." Daddy wouldn't let us put a sticker on the Ford or the jeep. "They're too hard to get off," he said.

The day after the Sugar Bowl, Daddy had mailed my third letter to Mr. Johnson, telling him that Rocky had figured out that "children" was the answer to the riddle.

Mama wore a worried look when she returned to the kitchen.

"What's the matter?" I asked.

"That was Mrs. Igou. Karen Isbell has been in a serious accident."

My eyes blurred with tears. "What happened? Is she okay?"

"She was hit by a car after school this afternoon. An ambulance took her to the hospital. One leg is broken pretty badly. Arlene said she also has a concussion, but the doctors believe she'll be okay in time."

"What's a concussion?" I asked.

"A head injury," Mama said softly.

Mark made a face. "That sounds painful."

"How long will she be in the hospital?"

"I don't know, sugar."

I didn't feel hungry anymore. Peanut butter stuck in my throat. When I could no longer hold back sobs, Mama held me and let me cry.

"Why . . . (snub, snub) . . . did God . . . let her . . . get hurt? Why . . . didn't . . . (snub) . . . He keep her safe? And why did He . . . let that mean ol' dog bite me?"

"Oh, sugar, bad things aren't God's fault."

"Then whose fault are they? He's the one with all the power and stuff."

Mama was quiet for a minute. She seemed to be gathering her thoughts. "When God made everything — the trees and birds and fish and cats and dogs and people — He looked over all that He has made and said it was very good."

I nodded, remembering the story from Sunday School.

"But not long after He made people, everything went terribly wrong, because the people He made, Adam and Eve, disobeyed Him. They sinned."

"Yeah, they ate that apple."

"When Adam and Eve sinned, that's when bad things started to happen."

I thought about nuclear bombs, biting dogs, broken legs, and concussions. "But can't God just fix everything?"

"Yes! He is fixing everything! It just takes a long, LONG time. Father God started fixing things and making everything right again when He sent His Son Jesus to earth to die on a cross and take the punishment for people's sins."

I sniffed. "Yes, ma'am."

"Each of us has to learn to trust Him — to trust His promises that we can't see over the troubles we do see. And you know what?"

"What?"

"God's right here with us right now."

I closed my eyes and imagined Jesus holding Mama and me. "Mama?"

"Yes, sugar?"

"I think Mr. Johnson would want to know about Karen's accident. Can I write him another letter?"

She kissed my forehead. "Yes, you may. I think that's a very good idea."

Dear Mr. Johnson,

I thought you would want to know that Karen had a bad accident. She was hit by a car. Her leg is broken, and she has a concussion. That means her head is hurt. It made me really sad. That's all I wanted to tell you.

Sincerely,

Jill Watson

P.S. The doctors think she'll be okay. Oh, and a dog bit me.

REFLECTIONS

A POINT TO PONDER

What was Mrs. Igou's bad news? Karen had been in a bad _____.

A PEARL FROM GOD

Jesus said, "I have told you these things, so that in Me you may have peace. In this world you will have trouble. But take heart! I have overcome the world." (John 16:33)

A PRINCIPLE TO LIVE BY

Even though Jesus loves you greatly, beloved, you will have troubles. Always remember, He is with you and will help you when troubles come. *"Don't be afraid, for I am with you; don't be discouraged, for I am your God. I will strengthen you and help you; I will hold you up with My victorious right hand." (Isaiah 41:10 NLT)*

Chapter 24:

Rocking Rocky Watson

"So humble yourselves under the mighty power of God,
and at the right time He will
lift you up in honor."
(1 Peter 5:6 NLT)

Rocky said that our coming to his basketball games made him nervous, but we still sneaked in from time to time. On the first Tuesday night of February, Daddy paid for two adults and two students at the ticket booth of the Fort Payne Wildcat/Fyffe Red Devil game. Daddy, Mama, Mark, and I crept up to the nosebleed section of the bleachers and hid in the shadows behind the hoop.

In the second quarter, Coach Ralph put Rocky in the game. I jumped up and hollered, "That's my brother!"

Mama tugged my shirttail. "Shhh! Jill, sit down and be still. You're going to embarrass Rocky if he hears you, and he'll never let us come again."

Between the excitement of getting another letter from Mr. Johnson that afternoon and Rocky's game, telling me to sit down and be still was like telling the moon not to rise.

Rocky's rebounding, defensive play, and a goal helped bring the Wildcats from a five-point deficit to a 37-34 lead at halftime. As his performance rose to higher heights over the third and fourth quarters, Daddy rose to his feet, hollering and cheering and grinning. I noticed that Mama didn't shush him.

Rocky had the game of his life — a payday for years of practice, patience, and perseverance. Jerry Whittle from the newspaper sat behind the Wildcats' bench, scribbling furiously.

Whittle's headlines of Thursday's sports section of the Times-Journal read:

"Watson Leads Ft. Payne Win."

"Rocking Rocky Watson came off the bench last Tuesday night and sparked the Fort Payne Wildcats to a 74-66 win over the Fyffe

Red Devils. Watson entered the game in the second quarter and helped bring the 'Cats from a five-point shortfall to a 37-34 lead at the half. He scored only one field goal, but his rebounding and defensive play were outstanding.

In the third and fourth quarters, Watson highlighted the Wildcat come-back in which they were down by as many as six points. He finished the night with a total of 14 points after scoring only 2 in the first half and hit 7 of 8 field goals mostly from the top of the circle.

The Red Devils jumped out front in the contest 24-15 and it looked as if they were off and running. However, Watson's appearance in the second stanza touched off a Fort Payne rally that ended when a Dick Groat set shot and Eddie Johnson's free throw gave the homestanding Wildcats a 37-34 lead at intermission.

Fyffe came back strong in the third period and Red Devil star Larry Lingerfelt dropped in a field goal with 5:35 left in the quarter to knot the count at 38-38. The visitors continued to improve with their spirited play and opened a six-point margin before Watson finally closed the gap and tied the score at 52-52 with a 35-foot set shot with only two seconds remaining in the third stanza.

Fort Payne's scoring balance paid off in the fourth frame as they dropped in 22 points while the Red Devils managed only 14.

Watson's performance overshadowed a fine game by Lingerfelt as the jumping jack from Fyffe scored an amazing total of 39 points to score over half of his team's total points. Larry was also a demon in the rebounding department as he dominated both backboards.

Fort Payne's fine showing brought words of praise from Coaches Ralph and Horton as both were well pleased with the Wildcats' scoring balance. They managed to put five men in double figures while the Red Devils had only two.

At the free throw line, the Wildcats were next to super as they hit on 24 of 28 for an 86 percent output.

Scoring for Ft. Payne: Johnson 19, Groat 17, Watson 14, Bud Davis 11, Jeff Davenport 10, Coker Mays 2, and Edward Houston 1.

For Fyffe: Lingerfelt 39, Roger Mashburn 10, Wendall Reynolds 8, Karl Abernathy 5, and Bynum 5."

Saturday morning, Rocky took Mark and me to the backyard, and under a basketball goal nailed to a hickory tree, he relived the game play by play. Mark was Eddie Johnson and passed Rocky the ball. I got to be a Fyffe Red Devil, jumping around, waving my arms, and trying my hardest to defend the goal. Rocky was the hero of that game, too.

REFLECTIONS

A POINT TO PONDER

Rocky practiced for _____ before the night of his big game.

A PEARL FROM GOD

"So let us not get tired of doing what is good. At just the right time, we will reap a harvest of blessing if we don't give up." (Galatians 6:9 NLT)

A PRINCIPLE TO LIVE BY

In the Bible, beloved, God tells us to work hard and never give up. First Corinthians 15:58 says: *"Always give yourselves fully to the work of the Lord, because you know that your labor in the Lord is not in vain."*

Chapter 25:

Where's Laura

"Then the LORD called to the man, 'Where are you?'"
(Genesis 3:9 NLT)

"Today was the best Valentine's Day ever!" I chirped as Mark and I piled into the Galaxy 500.

Mama smiled. "I'm glad. What made it so special?"

"They let Karen come to school for the Valentine's party, and I got to see her out in the hall and tell her that Mr. Johnson hopes she feels better soon. Jeanne Kellett pushed the wheelchair around the whole time and fussed over her like a mama hen over a little chick."

Mama laughed. "Well, I'm happy she had good help."

I opened my shoebox wrapped in red-foiled paper and paper-lace hearts. "And look at all these Valentines I got."

"Wow, that's a lot! How was your day, Mark?"

"Good."

169

"Did you get any Valentines?"

"One. Becky Killian made 'em for everybody. Nobody else in the eighth grade brought Valentines that I know of."

"Becky is so sweet," Mama said.

Mark showed me Becky's card. "Did you tell Karen the new clue?"

"No, I didn't get a chance, but I told her I'd call this afternoon. Is that okay, Mama?"

"Finish your homework first."

"I don't have any! Mrs. Robinson said it's a holiday and to just have fun."

Mark scowled. "Wish my teachers had said that."

"So, what did Mr. Johnson say in the letter?" Karen asked.

I sat on the rock hearth with the phone cord stretched from the telephone on the shelf under the shadowbox to the receiver at my ear. "He quoted a Bible verse and gave us another clue."

"What verse? What clue?"

"The verse is Jeremiah 16:19. Here, I'll read it to you: '*O LORD, my strength, and my fortress, and my*

170

refuge in the day of affliction.' And the clue says: Search the secret room for Jeremiah's next-door neighbor. There you'll find Jesurun and the secrets of Willow Springs."

Karen sighed. "How am I gonna do that when I can't even get up the stairs in this wheelchair?"

"We'll help you! If it's okay with your parents."

On Saturday, Karen opened the front door. "Hey, y'all come on in."

Mark helped her turn the wheelchair around and closed the door. "How's your leg?"

"It's okay. Still hurts a lot, but Daddy says I have to be patient. This kind of break takes a while to heal." She pulled a blue magic marker from under the cushion in the chair. "Y'all wanna sign my cast?"

Mark scribbled: "Get well soon, Mark Watson."

I wrote: "Get well soon, Love Jill," and drew a heart to dot the "i" in Jill.

Chuck skipped into the room. His face lit up like a Christmas tree when he saw Mark. He flexed both arms. "I'm strong!"

Mark felt his muscles. "My, what *big* muscles you have."

He grinned.

Mrs. Isbell came in behind him, frowning. "Karen, have you seen Laura?"

"No ma'am, not since . . . "

"Not since what?"

Karen looked down. "Uh . . . not since I told her she couldn't help us search the secret room 'cause she's too little."

Mrs. Isbell shook her head. "Oh, dear, I wonder where she's hiding."

She hides, too? I thought.

Mark took Chuck's hand. "Come on, hot-rod. Let's go outside and look for Laura."

Mrs. Isbell said, "Thank you, Mark. I'll go get Charles."

"I'll look upstairs." As I ran toward the staircase, I overheard Karen tell Mrs. Isbell, "I'm sorry, Mama. I didn't mean to hurt her feelings."

I searched my normal hiding places— under beds, behind the shower curtain, in closets — but no Laura. On my way back downstairs, I noticed the bookshelves were slightly ajar. I tugged *The Incredible Adventures of Professor Branestawn.*

Inside the secret room, Karen's little sister crouched in the corner by Mr. Johnson's signature. Her eyes were puffy and red. I dropped on the floor beside her. "Hey, Laura, whatcha' doing?"

She wiped her nose with the back of her hand. "Nothing."

"Did Karen hurt your feelings?"

She nodded.

"Well, she didn't mean to, and she's really sorry now."

"She is?"

"Uh huh."

Laura stared at the floor.

"Did you know that I'm the little sister in my family, too?"

"You are?"

"Yeah, I'm the youngest and the only girl and I have *two* big brothers. Sometimes they don't want me around, and it makes me feel sad. You know what I do when I'm sad?"

"What?"

"Hide."

"You do?"

"Yeah, but I always hope that somebody will come find me."

She nodded again.

"Being the little sister is a good thing, you know."

"Why?"

"'Cause your family watches out for you and tries to keep you safe. Did you know that everybody in the house is looking for you right now — even Karen."

"She is?"

I stood up and reached for Laura's hand. "She sure is. Come on, let's go get her and search this room together. We've got a mystery to solve."

Laura smiled.

REFLECTIONS

A POINT TO PONDER

When Laura's feeling got hurt, she _____.

A PEARL FROM GOD

"You know everything I do . . . You go before me and follow me. You place Your hand of blessing on my head. Such knowledge is too wonderful for me to understand. I can never escape Your Spirit! I can never get away from Your presence!" (Psalm 139:3-7 NLT)

A PRINCIPLE TO LIVE BY

Beloved, you can never hide from your loving heavenly Father. You are His child, and He watches over you at all times. He will never leave you. He will never abandon you. So, when you are sad, run to Him in prayer.

Chapter 26:

Who's Your Neighbor

"So, he asked Jesus, 'And who is my neighbor?'"
(Luke 10:29)

Mrs. Isbell and Mark carried the wheelchair up the stairs; Dr. Isbell carried Karen.

He kissed her forehead. "Okay, Karen-acy, have Mark come get me when you're ready to come back down."

"Yes, sir. Mama, will you stay and help us look?"

Mrs. Isbell smiled her sweet smile. "Of course."

Karen took Laura's hand. "And you, too, Laura?"

She nodded. "Okay."

Mark guided Karen's chair through the open bookcase. Mrs. Isbell glanced around the room. "So, children, what are we looking for?"

I pulled *National Velvet* from the bookshelf. "Jeremiah's neighbor."

"Jeremiah's neighbor. Hmm. Did Mr. Johnson tell you anything else?"

"He quoted a Bible verse," Mark said. "Jeremiah 16:19: *'O LORD, my strength, and my fortress, and my refuge in the day of affliction.'*"

Mrs. Isbell rubbed her chin thoughtfully. "Do you think there's a connection between that Bible verse and the clue?"

"Uh . . . the Bible verse is Jeremiah 16:19," I said.

"And the clue said to hunt for Jeremiah's neighbor," Karen said.

Mark drummed his fingers on the desk. "Hey, wait a minute. Jeremiah's neighbor. Where did Jeremiah live in the Bible, and who was his neighbor?"

Mrs. Isbell sat down. "Well, the book of Jeremiah is in the Old Testament. He was a prophet of God, and I think he lived near Jerusalem."

I snapped my fingers. "If he lived *near* Jerusalem, that makes Jerusalem his neighbor! Hurry! Let's look for something about Jerusalem."

Mark fanned through the Boy Scout Handbook. Karen rolled the wheelchair closer to the wall and studied Mr. Johnson's painting. Laura and I searched the children's classics on the shelves, and Mrs. Isbell rummaged through the desk drawer.

"Find anything?" Karen called over her shoulder.

Mark set the handbook on the desk. "Not yet."

Mrs. Isbell held up two pencils. "Found these, a paperclip, and a sucker as old as Methuselah. What about you, Jill?"

"No, ma'am, nothing here."

"Laura?"

She shook her head.

Mrs. Isbell said, "Let's think. Is there a book that might tell us about Jeremiah and Jerusalem?"

"Hey! I know! This one will." I grabbed the "J" encyclopedia and held it up. "The encyclopedia!"

REFLECTIONS

A POINT TO PONDER

In Mr. Johnson's next clue, he told us to look for Jeremiah's _____.

A PEARL FROM GOD

Jesus said, "Love your neighbor as yourself." (Matthew 22:39)

A PRINCIPLE TO LIVE BY

Beloved, do you know the two commandments most important to God? The first is love God. The second is love your neighbor as yourself. Who is your neighbor? Everyone around you is your neighbor. How do you love your neighbor? With acts of kindness, patience, forgiveness, encouragement, respect, helpfulness, and prayer.

Chapter 27:

Jeremiah's Neighbor

*"I have loved you with an everlasting love; I have drawn
you with unfailing kindness."*
(Jeremiah 31:3)

Mark took the heavy volume from me and hunted for Jeremiah. "Here he is. It says he was called the 'weeping prophet' and that he authored the books of Jeremiah, First and Second Kings, and Lamentations."

Karen's face fell. "That's all?"

"Yeah."

"Look up Jerusalem," I urged.

He flipped a few pages and read: "Jerusalem is in the Middle East between the Mediterranean Sea and the Dead Sea and is also known as the City of David. This beloved city of God has been destroyed twice, besieged twenty-three times, attacked fifty-two times, and captured and recaptured forty-four times. According to the Bible, King David conquered the city from the Jebusites and made it the capital of the kingdom of

Israel. His Son, King Solomon, built the first temple there."

I peered over his shoulder. "Anything about Jeremiah?"

"Nope."

"I have an idea," Mrs. Isbell said. "May I see that book, Mark?" She found the copyright page. "Children, where do you think the authors of the encyclopedia got most of their information about Jeremiah and Jerusalem?"

"From the Bible?" Laura asked in a small voice.

I nodded. "Yes, ma'am, probably the Bible."

"Hmm. The *Bible*," Mrs. Isbell said.

Silence.

"The Bible!!!" Karen shouted. "Laura, I think you're on to something!"

Mark pulled the old King James Bible from the bookshelf and eagerly ran a finger down the list of thirty-nine Old Testament books. "Psalms, Proverbs, Ecclesiastes, Song of Solomon, Isaiah, and here's Jeremiah — between Isaiah and Lamentations. It starts on page 705."

Karen gasped. "Wait a minute! Between Isaiah and Lamentations? Jeremiah's neighbors! Isaiah and Lamentations are Jeremiah's neighbors in the Bible!"

Mark's mouth dropped open. "You're right! Isaiah starts on page 655."

He fumbled through the pages.

"Hurry," I said.

"I'm trying!"

We held our breath.

"Here's Isaiah!" Mark began in chapter one, searching every page.

Chapter two.

Chapter three.

Chapter four.

Chapter five . . . and on and on he went. When Mark turned the page from chapter forty-three to chapter forty-four, he stopped. "Verses one through four are underlined in blue ink. And look!"

Wedged in the thin pages was a yellowed envelope addressed to "The Children of Willow Springs."

REFLECTIONS

A POINT TO PONDER

Mark learned that God's beloved city, Jerusalem, had been attacked _____ times.

A PEARL FROM GOD

"This is what the LORD of Heaven's Armies says, 'My love for Mount Zion is passionate and strong; I am consumed with passion for Jerusalem!" (Zechariah 8:2 NLT)

A PRINCIPLE TO LIVE BY

God loves Jerusalem. In Psalm 122:6, He said to pray for peace in Jerusalem and promised to bless all who love His city. Beloved, will you pray for peace in Jerusalem? Why not pray right now?

Chapter 28:

The Children of Willow Springs

"... *I will pour out My Spirit on your offspring,*
and My blessing on your descendants ..."
(Isaiah 44:3)

A holy hush shrouded the room.

"Oh, my goodness," Karen whispered. "The *children* of Willow Springs. Mr. Johnson's second clue. We found the secret!"

Tears filled Mrs. Isbell's eyes. "Mark, will you read those verses underlined, please?"

"Yes, ma'am. '*Yet now hear, O Jacob My servant; and Israel, whom I have chosen: Thus saith the LORD that made thee, and formed thee from the womb, which will help thee; Fear not, O Jacob, my servant; and thou, Jesurun, whom I have chosen.*'"

"Jesurun!" Karen's eyes darted to the mural.

Mark read on: "*For I will pour water upon him that is thirsty, and floods upon the dry ground: I will pour my spirit upon thy seed, and my blessing upon thine offspring:*

184

And they shall spring up as among the grass, as willows by the water courses."

I pointed to the inscription. "As willows by the water courses . . . just like Mr. Johnson's painting. What does the letter say?"

Mark held out the envelope. "Here, Mrs. Isbell, will you read it? I don't want to mess it up or anything."

Mrs. Isbell gently pulled out a tattered letter and read:

Dear Children,

Congratulations! You found the hidden room that Sister and I designed just for you. While working on Willow Springs Manor as a memorial to our dear parents, John F. and Mary Elizabeth Thomason, our hearts longed to honor them as well as leave a lasting legacy.

A legacy is something of value that you pass onto others after you are gone, and what better legacy to leave behind than a place of refuge for the children and future children of Willow Springs? This hidden room stands as a symbol of the secret place of your heart — your personal relationship with God. Psalm 91:1-2 tells us that "He that dwelleth in the secret place of the Most High shall abide under the shadow of the Almighty. I will say of the LORD, He is my refuge and my fortress: my God, in Him I will trust."

That's not to say that troubles will never come your way, dear ones. They undoubtedly will. But the trusting heart believes that God is ever watchful and with you in the midst of troubles."

I interrupted. "That's what Mama said."

"And your Mama's right," Mrs. Isbell agreed. She continued:

In Isaiah 44:1-4 (the verses underlined for you), God promised comfort and assurance for Jesurun (a poetical term

186

for Israel that means "beloved" or "one who is loved"), and He promised blessings for her children as well as the restoration of her land — a promise that, by the hand of God, Jesurun's children and land would thrive like willow trees beside a spring. It is our prayer, dear children, that God blesses you and that you flourish at Willow Springs.

Beloved, whenever you are glad or sad, mad or afraid, we pray that Father God will be your hiding place. May He bless you and keep you always, make His face shine upon you, be gracious unto you, and give you peace (Numbers 6:24-26).

Your friend,
Mrs. Eliza Thomason Snodgrass

P.S. If you trust God and His promises, please add your name, age, and the date below. You are welcome to leave something in this special room like *a book or letter or anything you feel will bless the children after you.*

I sat down. "So, God is with me all the time?"

Mrs. Isbell patted my hand. "Yes, Jill, He is."

"Then I'm done hiding. I don't have to be afraid anymore."

Laura smiled. "Me neither."

Karen said, "And God was with me when I had my accident."

Mrs. Isbell hugged her. "He most certainly was, honey, and He was with your daddy and me when we got the bad news that you were hurt."

We scanned the long list of names at the end of the letter — children who had lived at Willow Springs along with many others. On the second page toward the bottom, we found James Ralph Johnson, age 10, May 20, 1932. "My 10th birthday" was scribbled beside his name.

Karen pointed to the date in the corner. "Look, Mr. Johnson painted the wall seven years after he signed the letter."

Mark's eyes traveled from the wispy clouds in the mural to the bubbling brook. "Mr. Johnson must have added this painting to the room to bless kids like us." I could see the wheels turning in Mark's mind — imagining things that he might add to the secret room.

"Mama," Karen said, "may we write our names on the list?"

"Do you trust God and His promises?"

"Yes, ma'am," we answered.

"Then, of course you may." Mrs. Isbell stood. "I'll run get your daddy and Chuck. They'll want to see what you've found."

In the weeks that followed, the Isbells invited many children in our town to visit the secret room at Willow Springs. Mrs. Isbell told each visitor the story of God as our hiding place.

By summertime, Karen had graduated from the wheelchair to a cane; and by fall and sixth grade, she was racing around the playground again and running through the pastures of Willow Springs.

On a crisp Saturday morning in October, I walked toward Freddy and Steve's house looking for Mark. Birds sang in the treetops. Sunshine cut through the branches, painting shadow pictures on the ground. I paused at a patch of black-eyed Susans. "Welcome back, little flowers. I haven't seen you since fifth grade."

Suddenly, the Raymond's grumpy dogs charged — barking and baring sharp teeth. My mouth went dry. My heart galloped. I ran like the wind, frantically searching for Mark. The dogs tore after me.

I screamed, "Mark!"

Growls rumbled behind me. Tears stung my eyes. I couldn't see the boys anywhere and desperately hunted a tree to climb.

"Somebody, help!" I cried aloud but heard in my head, *God is your hiding place.*

I whipped around and, in the deepest voice I could muster, yelled, "*Git*!!! and leave me alone."

Stunned, both mutts froze. Tails tucked. I couldn't believe it!

Looking to the blue heavens, I raised a grateful thumbs-up. "Thank You, Lord Jesus!!!"

Wait till the boys hear about this, I thought and skipped away, singing at the top of my lungs:

"What have I to dread, what have I to fear,
Leaning on the everlasting arms?
I have blessed peace with my Lord so near,
Leaning on the everlasting arms.
Leaning on Jesus, Leaning on Jesus,
Safe and secure from all alarms . . . " [1]

The End

[1] LEANING ON THE EVERLASTING ARMS. Elisha A. Hoffman, 1817. Tune, Anthony J. Showalter, 1887.

AFTERWORD

Like my book, *The Adventures of the Lookout Mountain Gang: The Secret Chest*, *The Window at Willow Springs* is a mixture of facts, treasured memories, imagination, and a few tweaked dates.

The FACTS:

Karen Isbell Ivey and I became friends in 1965 in Mrs. Green's fourth grade class at Forest Avenue Elementary School. (And yes, she was hit by a car in the fifth grade.) Her parents, Dr. Charles Isbell and his wife, Barbara, owned Willow Springs for almost forty years — from the summer of 1968 (I used 1966 in the story) to 2005.

There was indeed an "extra" window at the Snodgrass/Isbell home that was visible from the driveway (not from the front of the house). The Isbells supposed the space was walled off during renovations before they moved in. Karen said, "There was a rather modern space heater in that bathroom in the vicinity of the window, so the previous owners may have closed it off to put the heater in."

The Palmer family purchased the home in 2005. Penny Palmer said that when they remodeled, the boarded-up space was opened. She joked that they had hoped to find a pot of gold but found only empty space.

Mrs. Eleanor Robinson at Williams Avenue School was one of my favorite teachers of all time. My answers to the questionnaire in the story were actually from a sixth-grade assignment in Miss Rains' classroom.

James Ralph Johnson was an accomplished author and artist born in Fort Payne, Alabama on May 20, 1922 to Judge James Andrew (Andy) and Vera Sue Small Johnson. He and my father, William Winfred Watson, attended DeKalb County High School together.

After retiring from a prestigious military career as a major in the United States Marine Corps, Mr. Johnson and his second wife, Burdetta F. Beebe (also a wildlife author) moved to New Mexico, where he focused on Western art and she continued writing.

My junior year at Fort Payne High School, my English teacher, Mrs. Sara Isbell Shipp (Karen's aunt), assigned a term paper on a well-known author. She gave me special permission to write about Mr. Johnson, and I corresponded with him throughout the fall of 1972. I saved his letters and the autographed copy of his survival book, *Anyone Can Live Off the Land.* Much of the contents of Mr. Johnson's letters in this story are his actual handwritten words.

Mr. Johnson died in 1997. Sadly, he never made the planned visit to our home atop Lookout Mountain, thus we never met face to face. As far as I know, Mr. Johnson's only connection to Willow Springs was in my imagination. A few years ago, I found an original James Ralph Johnson Western oil painting on eBay entitled *Afternoon* and purchased it.

The February 24, 1966 article about "Rocking Rocky Watson" by Jerry Whittle was found in the *Times-Journal* archives by my dear friends, Ben and Mary (Igou) Shurett. In reality, Rocky's big game happened his junior year, not senior.

Mrs. Isabell Lawrance taught eighth-grade math to my brothers, Rocky and Mark, as well as my husband, Phillip. Although she retired before my eighth-grade year, she taught my class as a substitute teacher on a few occasions.

Her son, William (Bill) Wise and his wife, Christiana, now live in the Summer Haven cottage where my mother and father honeymooned so many years ago. In a lovely phone conversation with Christiana, I learned that Bill's grandfather, Mr. Arthur Abernathy Miller, was a self-taught engineer that introduced electricity to northeast Alabama. He purposely traveled south to construct the dam on a watercourse that would not freeze in the wintertime. For rebar, Mr. Miller embedded railroad tracks into the bedrock for strength and durability, and for the dam's architectural design, he copied the flying buttresses from the Notre Dame Cathedral. The A. A. Miller Dam still stands above DeSoto Falls today. Christina also said that the family looked in pawn shops for years, hoping to find the stolen music box. Sadly, it was never recovered.

Since the time of this story, a great generation has passed on to glory. James Ralph Johnson. Mr. Dan Walker. Mrs. Lawrance. Jerry Whittle. Daddy died in 1994. Mama in 2003. Karen lost her mother in 2018 and her dad, Dr. Charles Isbell, on December 27, 2020. Four days later, Mrs. Eleanor Robinson, my fifth-grade teacher, went to heaven on New Year's Eve at the ripe old age of 97.

As I wrote this story last year amid Covid-19, civil unrest, hurricanes, and a rowdy presidential election, I asked the Lord, "What do You want this book to say to readers?" A passage from Psalm 32 came to mind:

"You are my hiding place;
You will protect me from trouble
and surround me with songs of deliverance.
I will instruct you and
teach you in the way you should go;
I will counsel you with My loving eye on you."

Beloved, whether glad or sad, mad or afraid, may the Lord Jesus Christ be your hiding place, and may you always trust in Him. May you learn to focus on His wondrous promises yet to come over the problems you face today. May He bless you and keep you forever; may the LORD make His face shine on you and be gracious to you; may the LORD turn His face toward you and give you everlasting peace.

Jill Watson Glassco